DETROIT
PUBLIC
LIBRARY

**Detroit Library for the Blind and
Physically Handicapped**
If you can only read Large Print, you
may be eligible to borrow audio books
through the mail at no cost to you.
For more information or to apply for
service:
Phone: 313-481-1702
Email: lbph@detroitpubliclibrary.org
Web: www.detroitpubliclibrary.org

DETROIT
PUBLIC
LIBRARY
Library on Wheels
3666 Grand River Ave.
Detroit, Michigan 48208
313-481-1706

D1444656

OCT - 2016

FOR THE LOVE OF YOU

This Large Print Book carries the
Seal of Approval of N.A.V.H.

FOR THE LOVE OF YOU

DONNA HILL

THORNDIKE PRESS

A part of Gale, Cengage Learning

GALE
CENGAGE Learning·

Farmington Hills, Mich • San Francisco • New York • Waterville, Maine
Meriden, Conn • Mason, Ohio • Chicago

GALE
CENGAGE Learning®

LIBRARY OF CONGRESS CATALOGING-IN-PUBLICATION DATA

Names: Hill, Donna (Donna O.), author.
Title: For the love of you / by Donna Hill.
Description: Large print edition. | Waterville, Maine : Thorndike Press, 2016. |
    Series: Lawsons of Louisiana | Series: Thorndike Press large print
    African-American
Identifiers: LCCN 2016020239 | ISBN 9781410491435 (hardcover) | ISBN 1410491439
    (hardcover)
Subjects: LCSH: African Americans—Fiction. | Large type books. | GSAFD: Love
    stories.
Classification: LCC PS3558.I3864 F674 2016 | DDC 813/.54—dc23
LC record available at https://lccn.loc.gov/2016020239

Published in 2016 by arrangement with Harlequin Books S. A.

This novel is lovingly dedicated to my dearest friend and mentor, Gwynne Forster. I miss you, my friend.

ACKNOWLEDGMENTS

I wish to thank my ever patient editor, Glenda Howard, for never giving up on me.

CHAPTER 1

The ten-hour flight from London Heathrow Airport landed in New Orleans, Louisiana, on time, to the delight of the weary passengers, Craig Lawson among them. His return home after more than ten years came with a mixture of regret and anticipation. Regret that for all those years he'd never felt compelled to return to the place where he'd grown up, and anticipation for the reason why he'd finally come home.

After breezing through customs and collecting his luggage, he and his business partner and lifelong buddy, Anthony Maxwell, headed for the pickup area and the car that awaited them. They passed a newsstand, and Anthony tapped Craig's arm and lifted his head in the direction of the magazines, where Craig's face graced the covers of *Entertainment Weekly, Variety* and *Black Enterprise.*

"If I didn't know you better, I'd think you

were important," Anthony teased.

Craig chuckled. "As long as the importance translates into success at the box office," he said. He took a last glance at the magazines and shook his head. When he'd broken ties with his family — his father, specifically — and headed to Los Angeles to pursue his dream as a screenwriter, it had been one of the most difficult things he'd had to do. To a Lawson, family was everything. Yet as hard as it was, looking back, he would not have done anything differently. As much as his father would like to believe that what he did for a living was nothing more than pandering, the real reason for his distaste for his son's profession went much deeper. Craig grew weary of fighting that ghost. So he left and never looked back. Now he was one of the most successful and celebrated screenwriters and movie directors on the East and the West Coasts. He had an Oscar, a Golden Globe and an NAACP Image Award under his belt. Behind closed doors he was called the golden boy. To his face he was Mr. Lawson.

As the duo exited baggage claim, they walked by the rows of drivers holding up signs with the names of their passengers. Craig's driver spotted him first and stepped out of the line.

"Mr. Lawson," the female driver greeted him with a tip of her head. "I'll get a cart for your bags."

Craig's right brow lifted in question, and he quickly assessed the stunning young woman in front of him. Even in her stark uniform of black slacks and jacket and a starched white shirt she was a work of art. The corner of his mouth curved ever so slightly as he watched her retrieve a luggage cart and return to them. Although he knew it was her job, the Southern gentleman in him wouldn't allow her to do it.

"Let me get the bags on the cart. We'll meet you at the car."

"I can take care of the bags, Mr. Lawson," she mildly protested.

"I'm sure that you can." He easily hoisted the oversize bags onto the cart. "But I'd rather that you didn't. My mama didn't raise me that way."

The young woman flushed, pressed her polished lips together and murmured a thank-you. "The car is this way." She started off toward the ground transportation area.

"Don't distract her from her driving," Anthony teased under his breath as they dutifully followed her to the exit.

"Not my intention. But I will say, it's a pleasure following her lead."

Truth be told, the last thing on his mind was getting with a woman. Although he had a reputation as a ladies' man, especially his leading ladies, it was all smoke and mirrors. The women who drifted in and out of his life were just that — transient. He found none that could excite his mind as well as his body, so he kept his relationships short, practical and amicable. For all of his numerous dalliances, there wasn't one woman who could say she had not been treated like a lady while she'd spent time with him.

"How does it feel to be back?" Anthony asked as they settled into the air-conditioned comfort of the town car.

Craig drew in a breath and glanced out the window as the Louisiana landscape unfolded in front of them. "Still trying to process it. Feels strange. I mean, things kind of look the same but different — smaller." He chuckled.

"You plan to see the family?"

Craig's jaw flexed. He leaned his elbow on the armrest and braced his chin on his fist. "I don't know. I'm sure they've heard that I'm back. Guess it wouldn't be right not to check in on my sister and brother and my cousins." He paused. "And I know that's not what you meant." He flashed his friend a look of censure. "I'm not going to see him."

Anthony held up his hands. "Hey, just asking a question, man."

Craig went back to staring out the window. The rift between father and son wasn't some simple spat that could be rectified with an adult conversation. His father made himself perfectly clear years ago that if Craig were to pursue "this trashy movie thing," he was cut off from the family and he didn't want him to set foot back in his house. His father, Jake Lawson, ran his family the way he ran his international land development enterprise — with an unbending hand. He couldn't — or rather wouldn't — see beyond his own narrow lens to be able to accept that his dreams and goals were not everyone else's. He kept Craig's sister, Alyse, and brother, Myles, on a short leash, but he never could control Craig. And Craig knew that his father's disillusionment with the Hollywood life ran deep, and his mother was at the root of it. But he wasn't his mother.

He pulled his cell phone out of his pocket and speed-dialed his location scout Paul Frazier.

"Yeah, Paul, we landed about an hour ago. In the car now, headed to the hotel. Look, I want you to be ready to take us over to the location when I arrive at the hotel. Yeah, I know I said tomorrow. I want to see it today. Cool. See you in a few." He disconnected the call.

"You don't want to chill for a while before going over there?" Anthony asked.

"Naw. I've seen pictures, and that's about it. I know Paul is good at what he does, but if I'm going to sink my money and a helluva lot of time and people's talent in this film, I want everything to be perfect. I'd rather find out sooner than later."

Jewel Fontaine took her cup of chamomile tea out to the back veranda of her sprawling pre–Civil War home. The house on Prytania Street, which was once a plantation, sat on five acres of land with a creek that ran the length of the property into the wooded area beyond. One of the former slave shacks still stood on the property, but it had been converted into an art studio when Jewel's career took off. Every time Jewel surveyed her home, she was infused with the spirits of her ancestors who'd toiled on this land and served in those rooms. As an artist she firmly believed in the sanctity of preserving the past for future generations. The constant work that had to be done for the upkeep of the Fontaine home and the cost of maintenance had all but drained her accumulated wealth from her art career, compounded with the care of her ailing father — she was on the precipice of being broke.

The idea that she might lose her home kept her up at night and dogged her steps during the day. She hadn't worked or sold a piece of art or sculpture in several years. She'd become disillusioned following her last poorly reviewed show nearly five years earlier, and then the decline of her father's health had turned her away from her passion. She refocused her energies on taking care of the man who had sacrificed everything for her. But in the past six months, she'd realized she couldn't do it alone, and she'd had to hire a live-in nurse. The cost was astronomical.

Then the call came, and like a miracle, her financial problems would be solved. CL Productions wanted to rent her home for the next six to eight weeks to shoot a film and was willing to pay an exorbitant amount of money for the privilege. She'd nearly leaped through the phone at the chance to lift the financial burden off her chest. The influx of cash would give her some breathing room and a chance to find other sources of revenue.

Jewel took a sip of her tea and gazed out

onto the midafternoon glory. The tight churning in her stomach had finally begun to ease.

"Ms. Fontaine!"

Jewel spilled her tea down the front of her floral sundress as she jumped up at the frantic call of her name, which could only mean one thing — *Daddy.* She ran across the main level and up the winding staircase. The sound of something crashing and shattering quickened her steps. She reached her father's bedroom door, and her heart stood still.

Craig didn't waste much time at the hotel. Now that he'd arrived in Louisiana, the adrenaline of his upcoming project pumped through his veins, making him more brusque and antsy than usual. He began spouting orders to his team the minute he walked into the suite. Within moments everyone was scurrying around like their jobs depended on it.

Less than a half hour after arriving, Craig, Anthony, Paul and his assistant, along with the photographer and driver, were heading to the Fontaine mansion.

"Why the rush?" Anthony asked again. "You generally don't get involved at this level."

Craig adjusted his shades on the bridge of his nose. "I have a bigger investment this time. I want everything to be on point and run like clockwork. No screwups. We don't have the usual wiggle room on time and cost overruns."

Anthony nodded his head. "Agreed." He clapped Craig on the shoulder. "You've done this countless times, bro," he said, lowering his voice. "This is going to be your best project yet. We got your back on this."

" 'Preciate that." He returned his attention to the script and line notes. The film chronicled a poor black family that rose from sharecropping to command the upper echelons of finance, real estate and politics, with great sex scenes and plenty of family drama and scandal thrown in. He wondered if his family would recognize themselves in the characters. Of course, he'd changed names and some professions to suit the storyline.

The driver turned the black Suburban onto a winding road that led to the Fontaine mansion. According to his location scouts' notes, the home had once been a plantation and one of the shacks that had housed former slaves on the expansive land still remained. When the home appeared and spread out in front of him, it was like being thrown back into time to the days of *Gone With the Wind.* The only thing missing was the Confederate flag. The SUV came to a stop.

Craig got out and fully took in the setting, already beginning to visualize the scenes and where they would take place. It was better than any description or photograph could capture. This was exactly the setting he wanted. What he needed to do now was meet the owner and set up the official working arrangement. Generally this was something that Paul handled, but this project was his dream movie. It was his first time at bat as writer, director *and* executive producer. He had a lot riding on this and knew that there were plenty who wished him well and an equal amount that couldn't wait to see him fail.

"Anthony and Paul, come with me. You guys can wait here," he said to the photographer and Paul's assistant. He flipped a page on his clipboard. *Jewel Fontaine.* It sounded like the name of someone that would live in a house like this. He strode down the pathway that led to the palatial entrance. The front was framed by six white columns, three on each side of the double front door. It was two levels with a wraparound terrace on the second floor and paneled windows.

Craig led his small entourage up the three steps to the front door. He rang the bell and made a mental note to have a temporary door knocker installed for the film.

Moments later the door opened and a woman dressed in what appeared to be a nurse's uniform stood in front of them.

"Can I help you?"

"Craig Lawson. Ms. Fontaine?"

"No. I'm . . . Ms. Fontaine is busy right now. It may be best if you come back."

"No. I don't think that would be best. I'd appreciate it if you could get Ms. Fontaine. Please let her know that Craig Lawson is here to talk with her about the film."

The woman in white huffed and rolled her eyes. "If you go round back, I'll ask Ms. Fontaine to meet you there."

"Thank you," Craig said, his tone softening to match the smile on his lips.

"I'll get Ms. Fontaine," she said, her tone decidedly changed.

Craig turned and got a quick *I told you so* look from Anthony. He ignored it.

The trio rounded the building and found themselves in a mini paradise.

"You did good, Paul," Craig said, slapping him heartily on the back.

"Thanks, boss. Ron was the one that actually found it," Paul said of his assistant.

Craig pressed his lips together and nodded. What he appreciated about his staff was that they never hesitated to spread their support and share the credit. He set the clipboard down on a circular white metal table that was shaded by a huge umbrella. There was a half cup of tea on the table and a newspaper that had fallen to the ground. He reached down, picked it up and placed it back on the table. He turned at the sound of a door opening behind him.

The woman didn't simply walk through the door. She swept in like a character from a novel. Every nerve in Craig's body vibrated. Like the filmmaker that he was, he cataloged every inch of her, from the riotous swirl of cinnamon curls that seemed to want to break free from the knot on the top of her head to the high cheeks, wide expressive honey-toned eyes, sleek arching brows and full pouty lips all set on a flawless canvas of nut brown. The loosely flowing sundress that bared her shoulder and reached her ankles did nothing to camouflage the curves beneath.

Jewel stopped in front of him. "Mr. Lawson?"

"Yes. And you must be Ms. Fontaine." He extended his hand.

Jewel placed her hand in his, and Craig felt the heat of their contact race straight to his groin. He shifted his stance slightly and cleared his throat to give himself a moment to recover.

"Thanks for seeing me."

"You didn't give me much choice, Mr. Lawson."

"You're right. I realize you were expecting me — us — tomorrow, but I wanted to see the estate for myself and meet you as soon as possible. I hope we can talk for a few minutes, go over the details and work out the schedule."

Jewel lifted her chin ever so slightly, a move that Craig had seen his sister use whenever she was ready to do battle. He reflexively clenched his jaw. Craig glanced over his shoulder and angled his body. "Ms. Fontaine, this is my business partner and a producer of the film, Anthony Maxwell."

Anthony stepped in between the standoff and extended his hand. "Pleasure to meet you, Ms. Fontaine. Your home is better than any pictures."

She offered up a hint of a smile. "Thank you." She turned her attention to Craig, and he felt her stare right in his center. "We need to talk, Mr. Lawson."

His radar went on full alert, and every

instinct told him that this was not going to go well. "Of course."

Jewel stepped down off the back porch and walked toward the brook that ran behind the house. Craig fell in step next to her and wondered what that incredible scent was that floated around her.

"Mr. Lawson —" She stopped and turned to him, and he was hit in the chest again by the depth of her eyes. "I don't know how to say this, but —" She paused, looked at the water and then at him. "I'm going to have to back out of this arrangement."

He'd expected a discussion about more money, no Mondays or eating in the kitchen, or whatever other quirky thing homeowners wanted when they rented out their property, but not this.

Craig bent his head toward her in an almost combative move. "Excuse me?"

"I've changed my mind. This may be a great opportunity, but it will be too disruptive and . . . I can't allow this." She folded her arms beneath the swell of her breasts. "I'm sorry," she said softly.

Craig was totally thrown. It took him a minute to process what she was saying. Months of work would go down the drain; the time it would take to find a new location would cost thousands and set the production schedule back by any number of days, possibly weeks. As the scenario played in his head, his level of pissed off rose. He'd never been one to take no for an answer, and now wasn't the time to get started.

"Listen —" He reached out to touch her, and the instant his fingertips touched her bare arm he knew it was a major mistake. What felt like electricity brushed across his skin. "I, uh, totally get it that having a film crew in your home is a pretty big imposition." He gave her his best Oscar-winning smile, coated with Nawlins drawl. He held up his hands. "I promise you we will totally respect your home. Whatever rules you set down . . . that's what it will be."

He watched the pink tip of her tongue peek out and stroke her bottom lip. He swallowed.

"It's much more complicated than that, Mr. Lawson," she said softly, the hard stance that she'd taken earlier seeming to ease somewhat. "I deeply apologize for any inconvenience —"

"If it's about money, we can work that out. It's a big imposition, and you should be compensated accordingly."

"What makes you think I need or want your money!" Her hands dropped to her sides, and her fingers curled into her palms.

The 360 in her tone and body was so sudden, Craig actually took a step back. "I wasn't trying to imply that you did," he said, keeping his voice low and even in the hope of rescuing this rapidly sinking ship. "I'd really like to talk this out. I'm sure we can do whatever it is that you need to be comfortable."

Jewel slowly shook her head. Her lids fluttered rapidly, and her nostrils flared even as she turned her lips inward and tightened them.

Craig took a cautious step closer. There were two things he was really good at: finding movieworthy material and noting the warning signs in a woman's face. *This* woman was on the verge of tears, and he was pretty sure that it had nothing to do with the film, at least not directly.

"I'm sorry," she managed and stuck out her hand.

Craig's gaze ran over her face, but she wouldn't look directly at him. He took her hand and slowly let his fingers envelop hers. "Thank you, Ms. Fontaine. I'm sorry that things didn't work out. If you change your mind, you have the number."

She bobbed her head, and he released her hand, turned and headed back to where he'd left Anthony.

"Let's go," he snapped, storming past Anthony.

Anthony double-timed it to catch up. "Yo, what happened?"

Craig slid on his shades. "We'll talk back at the hotel and Paul can start looking for a new job."

By the time the crew returned — very subdued — to the hotel, Craig's ire had diminished by a fraction. At least he'd stopped cussing and tossing death stares at his crew.

"Look," Anthony said, pulling Craig off to the side once they'd entered the suite, "go easy. We've been in tighter situations. We have some alternate locations on tap. We'll find the right venue and keep it moving. Every one of us has screwed up at some point," he added with a knowing look.

Craig grunted. "Yeah. I know. It's just when you feel something in your gut . . ." He let his words drift away and wondered if he meant the location or Jewel Fontaine. He clapped Anthony on the arm. "You're right. We'll work it out." He slung his hands into his pants pockets and turned to the crew, whose gazes were glued to the floor.

"Okay, look . . . it appears that we're not going to be able to use the Fontaine location for the shoot. For whatever reason, the lady of the house has changed her mind." He tossed a look in Paul's direction.

Paul shifted his weight and looked appropriately contrite.

"Mr. Lawson . . ."

Craig turned his attention toward Diane Fisher, one of the assistant location scouts. "Yes?"

She cleared her throat, glanced briefly at Paul then focused on Craig. She lifted her dimpled chin. "It wasn't Paul's fault. He gave me my first assignment. I should have had her sign the contract." She swallowed. "I didn't. I guess I was a little starstruck when I realized who she was. I'm sorry. But this isn't Paul's fault."

Craig held back a smile. He admired loyalty among his friends and his working crew. It was clear to him, however, that there was just a little something more than work between Paul and Diane, which was cool as long as it didn't interfere with the job. He'd give them both a pass on this one.

"Thank you for telling me that, Diane. You'll know for next time."

The wave of relief in the room was palpable. There would be a next time instead of a goodbye.

"In the meantime I want Paul and Diane

to get busy with the secondary locations. We can't afford to have this project fall behind schedule." He paused. "Thanks, y'all." He tugged in a breath and exhaled. "I know how hard you work, and you're some of the best in the business. I don't say it much, but I appreciate each of you." He turned and walked into his adjoining room, totally missing the look of outright shock on the faces of his crew.

Craig closed the door to his room and crossed the plush carpeted floor to the mini-bar. He poured himself a shot of bourbon on the rocks. He took a deep, satisfying swallow and allowed the smooth liquor to seep into his veins, warming them before he went to stand in front of the floor-to-ceiling window. His eyes cinched at the corners while he rocked his jaw from side to side and looked out on the city that he'd once called home. Had anyone asked him a year ago if he would ever return, he would have said, "Hell, no." But here he was, back home, doing the very thing that had sent him away in the first place. He snorted a laugh at the irony of it all. The prodigal son had returned. By now his father would know that he was back. Why did it still matter?

He turned away from the past, crossed back to the bar and refilled his shot glass. Jake Lawson had been very clear when Craig announced that he was uninterested in learning about, participating in or ultimately running his father's global real estate firm. As far as Jake Lawson was concerned, Craig was on his own, cut off from the family.

It had been ten years, and though he would never admit it, even with all the success he'd attained since he'd left, what he missed was his father and his blessing on all that he'd accomplished. What hurt him the most was not understanding his father's near irrational disdain for Craig's chosen profession. Growing up, Jake had instilled in each of his children the belief that they could achieve anything that they wanted in this world — apparently as long as it was what Jake Lawson wanted his children to achieve.

Wallowing in self-pity and reflection was never Craig's MO, and he didn't plan to start now. What he needed to concentrate on was getting his movie filmed and produced. His work was what was important. It was his validation. Nothing else mattered.

His thoughts shifted to his meeting with Jewel Fontaine. She'd flat-out told him no.

No was a word that never sat well with him. If he didn't take it from his father, he wouldn't take it from her, either. Everyone could be persuaded. Everyone had a button that could be pushed. He simply had to discover what her yes button was.

He tossed back the rest of his drink, a plan formulating in his head. He smiled. Tomorrow was another day. He might have lost the first battle, but the fight was far from over.

The house was blissfully quiet. Jewel walked out onto the back veranda and sat on a cushioned lounge chair. She placed her cup of tea on the table beside her and tucked her feet beneath her. The sound of cicadas peppered the night, and the scent of lavender from her garden helped to soothe her unsettled soul. Her nerves were still on edge, a combination of the unannounced visit by Craig Lawson and her father's latest episode. It was hard to distinguish which event had the greater effect on her. Meeting Craig Lawson had had a visceral impact. She felt as if every sense, every nerve was suddenly jolted awake when they met eye to eye and he took her hand. It still seemed to tingle. But that was silly. It was no more than her overwrought emotions at work.

Then there was her father. Her heart ached as if it had been pounded and abused then shoved back into her chest. Watching the man that she loved, admired and worshipped slowly disappear was, on some days, more than she could manage. Today was one of those days.

Jewel got up from the lounge chair and walked over to the railing that embraced the veranda. She gazed out on the star-filled night. If only she could cast a wish upon a star. She would wish that she had her career back. She would wish that she had her father back, and she would wish that Craig Lawson had never entered her life to remind her of what she'd left behind.

The choices and sacrifices she'd had to make over the past few years had begun to pile upon her soul, weighing it down, an anchor determined to tug her into the depths of no return.

Her stomach twisted with resentment and the guilt of it. She had no right to feel those emotions. But she did. She begrudged the world that had turned its back on her. She cursed fate that had leveled its will upon her father and locked them both in a spinning cycle of decline.

She sighed heavily and searched out the heavens for a star. If only it were that easy.

In another six months, she would lose the home she'd grown up in. She'd lose the ability to take care of her father. Opportunity had knocked today — literally — and yet she couldn't let it in. What was she going to do?

CHAPTER 2

Jewel had spent a sleepless night tossing and turning as dozens of unattainable scenarios played in a loop inside her head. Finally giving up on sleep, she rose with the sun, checked on her father to find him comfortably sleeping, and then puttered around in the kitchen, determined to find a solution to her untenable situation.

Making something always seemed to help clear her thoughts. Had it been at an earlier phase of her life, she would have been found in her studio, sculpting her next piece of art or creating her next abstract on canvas. She couldn't remember when she'd last molded a piece of clay or chiseled granite or stroked vibrant colors with a paintbrush. Instead her hands and her mind realigned themselves and found a new purpose in baking. The same artistry that she'd used in her work transferred itself to create unique and sumptuous cakes, pies, cookies and muffins.

She sold some of her confections to a local baker from time to time and had even prepared one-of-a-kind wedding cakes. Minerva, her father's home attendant and Jewel's pseudoconfidante, had for the past year been encouraging her to pursue her baking — take it to the next level, build a business, she'd said. But Jewel couldn't. She was an artist — at one time a renowned artist who traveled the world and held standing-room-only launches in galleries here in the States and abroad. Baking was a poor second cousin, an outlet for her idle hands and nothing more.

Today felt like a blueberry muffin day, she reasoned, and while the house remained under the blanket of slumber, Jewel created her other brand of magic.

By the time the sun was in full bloom, Jewel's kitchen was filled with the warmth and aroma of a high-end bakery. She eased the tray from the oven and placed it on the counter to cool then prepared a pot of chamomile tea. With her cup of tea, she took a plate with a muffin and homemade jam to the veranda and picked up the newspaper en route.

Nestled in her favorite spot, she opened the paper and was hit in the center of her being by the virile image of Craig Lawson, whose face graced the cover with the caption New Orleans Prodigal Son Returns.

The two-page article went on to talk about his meteoric rise in the movie industry and of course the iconic Lawson family, of which he was a part. It hinted at a rift between father and son, but the details were sketchy, giving way to more questions than answers. The one steady theme was that his return and the ensuing project would bring business to the city, as the article indicated that Lawson was a staunch supporter of employing local talent for his projects.

"A regular saint," Jewel murmured around a mouthful of muffin. She washed it down with a healthy swallow of tea.

She gazed off into the distance. *Craig Lawson.* He was like many of the stars that peppered his films — larger than life. There was a magnetic pull about him, a swagger and self-assurance that was nearly impossible to resist. She'd felt it when they faced each other, when he clasped her hand in his. She'd felt herself become trapped in the undertow of his dark eyes, and it had taken all that she had to pull herself free. But at what cost?

"There you are."

Jewel glanced up and over her shoulder and smiled. "Good morning."

"I see you've been busy." Minerva stepped fully onto the veranda.

"A little." She laughed, but then her expression turned somber. "How's Dad?"

"Resting. I'm going to get him his breakfast shortly. I know he'll be happy to get one of your famous muffins to go with it."

"Hmm." She lowered her gaze.

Minerva sat down next to Jewel and placed a comforting hand on her knee. "There are going to be bad days," she said softly. "You can't let it overwhelm you. And . . . as hard as it is for us to accept, there will be more bad days than good."

Jewel dragged in a breath. "I know," she whispered. She turned to Minerva. "I'm scared, Minny."

"Of course you are. But it's going to be all right. It will. What you have to do is remember that and be the strong woman that he raised you to be. That's what he needs now."

Jewel slowly shook her head. "I don't know if I can. We're going broke, and fast. How will I take care of him, this house — you?"

Minerva frowned. "I thought you were going to let them do the film. They were willing to pay a pretty big sum, from what I remember you telling me."

"I turned them down."

"Why on earth would you do that?"

"After yesterday's episode with Dad, I realized that it would be too much for him, too much disturbance. I couldn't risk that."

Minerva was pensive for a moment. "Is that the real reason?"

"What do you mean? Of course it is. What other reason could I have?"

"Maybe it's because *you* aren't ready to reconnect with the world or forgot how. Your father has withdrawn — and not by choice. You, on the other hand, decided to live this life."

"He's my father! What choice did I have?"

"Taking care of your father is one thing — not living your own life is quite another." She pushed up from her spot and looked down at Jewel. "It's your decision. Make sure you come to it for the right reason. Your father is going to go through what he will go through whether you let them film here or not." She patted Jewel's stiff shoulder and walked back inside the house.

Jewel glanced at the confident face of Craig Lawson staring up at her from the newspaper, almost as if he was challenging her. Was Minerva right? Was it her father that she was trying to protect — or herself from the soul-stirring attraction she felt for Craig Lawson?

While his team scrambled to get the project back on track and into his good graces, Craig headed out. He was unaccustomed to not getting what he wanted when he wanted it. He never allowed anything or anyone to stop him cold — Jewel Fontaine would not become the exception. Everyone had a price, something that could be bargained for. All he needed to do was find out what Jewel's something was. He fastened his seat belt, put the Suburban in gear and pulled out of the hotel garage.

As he cruised along the streets of New Orleans, the landscape of his youth unfolded in front of him. A great deal had changed since he was last here. Signs of gentrification were evident everywhere that he looked, from the small neighborhood shops that had transformed into internet cafés and outdoor eateries to the once debilitated homes that were in the throes of restoration. He was sure it was great for business — but whose business, and where did the people that once owned and lived here go? That was the story that he wanted to tell, the real history of his home and the people who made it.

His dashboard lit with an incoming call.

He pressed the phone icon, and Anthony's voice came through the speakers.

"Yeah, Tony, what's up?"

"Where did you go off to?"

"I'll tell you about it when I get back."

"Paul and Diane are out scouting the alternate locations. I should have some news this afternoon."

"All right. Stay on it. I'll be back to the hotel in a couple of hours."

"You're going to see Ms. Fontaine, aren't you?"

Craig bit back a smile. He never could hide much from Anthony. "I'll talk to you later."

"Why are you so dead set on this place? I know it fits the specs, but there are plenty of places to choose from without having to twist the owner's arm to do it. So I know there has to be another reason."

"I don't like being told no. Reason enough?"

"If you say so. Just know that I know you, and I know better. Good luck."

He snorted a laugh. " 'Preciate it." He disconnected the call.

Anthony was right. It wasn't as cut-and-dried as being told no, even though that was a big part of it. If he would allow himself a moment of honesty, he would admit that the real reason was that he wanted to see her again. See if on the morning after, she still managed to seep into his pores and flow through his veins. Best way to do that was face-to-face. He took a quick glance at the folder on the passenger seat. The documents inside, once signed, would give him access to the mansion *and* Jewel Fontaine for the next two months. He had no plans to return to the hotel empty-handed again.

The ride over to the Garden District, where Jewel lived, was about a twenty-minute ride from the center of town. Her home was on the edge of the district, set back and away from the street in a cul-de-sac that separated it from view of other homes in the area, which was ideal for the project.

He made his approach to the Garden District. This historic location was home to some of the most iconic mansions in the state, all of which had been plantations during slavery. Anne Rice, of vampire fame, had a house there, along with the likes of football giant Peyton Manning, who grew up in the district.

Craig turned onto Prytania Street, which was lined with homes in the Gothic style. He reached the end of the lane and turned down the winding path that led to the

Fontaine home. An unexpected knot of anxiety suddenly twisted in his gut when the mansion came into view. Or was it anticipation?

He took the path slowly and came to a stop at the top of the line of trees that umbrellaed the grounds. He turned off the ignition. For a few moments, he sat in the car, staring at the old-world majesty of the home and imagining the rich history that slept behind the walls and wafted among the rafters. What did the beautiful and difficult Jewel Fontaine add to that picture?

Craig snatched the folder from the passenger seat, got out and strode purposefully toward the sweeping entrance. Just as he put his booted foot on the first step of the landing, the double front door opened.

Jewel stood framed in the doorway, a mixture of past grandeur and present-day class.

Craig didn't realize that he'd actually frozen mid-step until she spoke his name.

"Mr. Lawson. I wasn't expecting you."

He couldn't tell from her even tone if her words were a reprimand or ones of pleasant surprise. He climbed the three steps until he was inches in front of her. Something soft and inviting spun around her in the morning breeze — her scent combined with the aroma of fresh baking that drifted to him from the interior of the house.

Craig cleared his throat, suddenly unsure of what he wanted to say. "Um, good morning, Ms. Fontaine. I apologize for not calling."

She didn't budge, a sentinel protecting her domain.

"What can I do for you? I thought we concluded our business yesterday."

"I was hoping that we could talk."

"About?"

He ran his tongue lightly across his dry lips. "The house."

Her lids lowered ever so slightly over her deep brown eyes, then she looked directly at him. She tipped her head slightly to the side. Her right brow rose. "Have you had breakfast?"

For a moment he was thrown. It was the last thing he'd expected her to say. "Actually, no. I haven't."

She drew in a short breath, opened the door farther and stepped to the side. "Come in."

Craig walked past her. Her scent clouded his thoughts.

Jewel shut the door. "This way." She led him through the large foyer that was appointed with an antique hall table upon which sat an oversize glass vase filled with lilies. On the walls hung several oil paintings that he recognized as her work. The highly polished wood-plank floors gleamed with their reflections and echoed their footsteps. She made a short right turn, and the space opened onto a kitchen that rivaled any master chef's.

Every size pot and pan hung from black iron ceiling hooks over a polished-cement island counter that boasted a sink and a six-burner stove with cabinetry beneath. The far end of the island was for seating. The double oven and restaurant-size stainless steel refrigerator were in sharp contrast to the perfectly restored potbellied stove that sat like a Buddha at the far end of the kitchen.

"Coffee or tea?"

Craig blinked. "Coffee. Please."

"Have a seat." She went to the overhead cabinets and took out a bag of imported Turkish coffee and prepared it. Within moments the scent of fresh-brewed coffee mixed with the tempting aroma of the blueberry muffins that sat in a cloth-lined basket, waiting to be devoured. She took out a plate and retrieved jam and whipped apple butter from the fridge and placed them both on the table.

"You have an incredible home."

"Thank you." She poured his coffee and brought it to the table. "Cream, milk, sugar?"

"I take it black. Thanks."

Jewel took a seat opposite him. "Help yourself to a muffin if you want. They're fresh."

His eyes narrowed. "You didn't make these?"

"Actually, I did."

The corner of his mouth lifted in a grin. "A woman of many talents." He reached for a muffin and put it on his plate. "I noticed your artwork out there. Stunning." He cut the muffin in half and slathered it with apple butter. He glanced up when she didn't comment. He took a thoughtful bite and experienced heaven. His eyes closed in appreciation. "Wow, this is incredible." That brought a smile to those luscious lips of hers.

"I learned to bake from my grandmother, right here in this kitchen. It slowly became a passion of mine over the years."

"So you grew up here?"

"The house has been in the family for almost four generations, dating back to the emancipation. I lived here with my grandmother and my father until I graduated high school."

Where was her mother in the scenario? He didn't recall reading anything about her. "You attended the Sorbonne."

Her eyes flashed. A curious smile curved her mouth. "Have you been reading up on me? I thought it was the house you were interested in."

Both, he wanted to say but didn't. "Any time I'm in negotiations with anyone I want to know as much as possible about them."

"I see." Her lips narrowed.

"If I remember correctly, the original owner, Charles Biggs, was one of the few owners of these homes that didn't own slaves."

"True. My great-great-grandparents worked here and earned a wage. They were free blacks. They lived in the house in the back. When the owner died, he left the house, the land, everything to my great-great-grandparents." She huffed. "It didn't sit well with the neighbors." Her gaze drifted off. "My granddad told me stories about how my greats fought off threats both physical and emotional from the landowners around here. Nothing worked, and eventually they came to respect my family."

"Lot of history here," he said respectfully and struggled to contain his surprise and excitement about the eerie similarities of

44

their ancestors.

"Yes, there is." She stared into her cup of tea. "So why are you here, Mr. Lawson?" She leveled her gaze on him, and something warm simmered in his belly.

"I believe that if you hear me out, you'll change your mind about renting out your home."

Jewel seemed to study him for a moment, as if the weight of her reality pressed against her shoulders, and with a breath of apparent acceptance she said, "Let's talk out back." She led the way to the veranda.

"Please, have a seat," Jewel said, extending her hand toward one of the cushioned chairs.

"Thanks." Craig sat and placed his plate and cup on the circular white wrought-iron table.

Jewel sat opposite him, adjusted her long skirt and leaned back. She folded her slender fingers across her lap. "So . . . I'm listening."

Craig cleared his throat, focusing on Jewel, and for a moment talking about the project was the last thing on his mind. He shifted his weight in the chair. "I believe as an artist you can fully appreciate a project of passion." Her nostrils flared ever so slightly as if bracing for attack. "That's what this project is for me. Everything that I've done and everything that I have accomplished has led me here — now." He pushed out a breath. "It's the story of my family, the Lawsons."

Her lashes fluttered, but her features remained unreadable.

"Of course, I've changed the names, to protect the guilty," he said, not in jest. "The story of a family that came from nothing, with a history of rising up from slavery, starting a business in a shack and building a legacy that led all the way to the seats of power in Washington." He leaned forward, held her with his gaze.

"More important," he continued, his voice taking on an urgency, "is that *now* is the time. With all that is going on in the world, with all that is happening to black lives, this is a story not only of history but of hope. It's about resiliency, about who we are as a people and all that we can be." He took a breath. "From what you told me about your family, we —" he flipped his hand back and forth between them "— have a helluva lot in common. This house, this land and the history of it is the ultimate backdrop for the telling of this story. It won't only be my family story, but your family story as well."

Jewel pushed up from her seat and walked over to the railing to gaze out at the rolling slopes. "I know about your work. I've read the reviews and the write-ups." She turned to face him. "They all say good things — that you are brilliant." She smiled faintly. "And that in an industry that is utterly jaded, you still keep your integrity intact and you never work on a project for the money but for the passion."

Craig took the comments in stride. He got up and stood beside her. He felt her stiffen. "I've read all about you, too." Her eyes widened for an instant. "You're one of the most influential artists of your generation. But suddenly you all but vanish from the public eye. Don't you miss it? Do you still paint, sculpt?"

"In answer to all of your questions, no, I don't," she practically whispered.

He watched her throat work as if she would reveal more, but she didn't. If he knew nothing else about artists of any medium, they weren't fulfilled if they didn't do what they were born to do. But instead of saying what he thought, he said, "If it's about the money, we are more than willing to pay twice what we offered, and I —"

Jewel spun her body toward him so quickly that it forced him to take a step back. Her eyes narrowed in fury.

"You think because I'm not in the lime-light that I'm some kind of charity case and that I *need* your money!"

He reached out and gently placed his hand on her arm. "I'm sorry. That's not what I meant. All I'm saying is that I understand that it is an imposition, that strangers would interfere with your regular routine for weeks and you should be duly compensated, not to mention that your home would be the centerpiece of an amaz-ing film. That's all worth something, and for me, having this film made at this loca-tion is more valuable than you could imag-ine." A slow, endearing smile curved his mouth while his eyes danced across her face.

Jewel, by degrees, seemed to relax her body. She lowered her head for a moment then looked directly at him, and the con-nection was so intense that he felt as if he'd been hit in the gut.

"Okay," she finally said. "You can shoot your film here."

A smile like hallelujah broke out on his face. He totally kicked protocol to the curb, grabbed her around the waist and spun her in a circle. She laughed like a kid at Christ-mas, and it was pure music.

He finally set her on her feet, and they

were but a breath apart. He saw the flecks of cinnamon in the irises of her eyes, felt the warmth of her body, the beat of her heart. He wanted to know what her lips felt like, to taste her . . . just a little.

"Sorry," he said.

Jewel gazed at him while the shadow of a smile hovered around her mouth.

"Thank you," he said, "and I swear we'll make this as painless for you as possible."

"I'm going to hold you to that, Mr. Lawson."

"I think maybe you can call me Craig."

The tip of her tongue brushed across her bottom lip. "Jewel."

"I'll have some new paperwork drawn up and sent over first thing tomorrow," Craig said as they walked to the front door.

They stood side by side on the landing.

"Fine. Can I ask you something?"

"You can ask me anything," he said, still euphoric over the positive turn of events.

"If this place and your family's legacy are so important to you, why did you stay away for ten years?"

The question seemed to take him off guard. For a moment he didn't respond, but he quickly regained his composure. "How about this . . . I promise to tell you all about it if you agree to have dinner with

49

me, to thank you."

Jewel swallowed and took a small step aside. "I don't think so."

"Lunch?" He covered the step she'd given up. He faced her. "Starbucks on the corner of wherever," he joked.

Jewel laughed. "Fine. Lunch," she conceded.

"Tomorrow. One o'clock. I'll come and get you." He jogged down the three steps. "Enjoy your day," he said over his shoulder.

Jewel stood on the porch landing until the Suburban was long out of sight. Why had she agreed to have lunch with him? Why had she agreed to have his film crew in her home? Why was her heart racing as if she'd run a marathon, and why did she feel as if the lights had suddenly come on after much too long in the darkness? She turned and walked back inside. Craig Lawson was the answer to all of her questions.

CHAPTER 3

Craig was light on his feet as he crossed the threshold to the suite reserved for the crew. Since their arrival his team had transformed the lush two-bedroom suite into a functioning production space with a splash of elegance. His spirits soared even higher when he saw that everyone was already up and at it.

Anthony glanced up from the computer screen when Craig walked in. "Hey, man." He gave him a questioning look.

Craig gave him a thumbs-up and a satisfied grin. "It's a go."

Anthony slowly shook his head in amazement. "I want details."

Craig nodded then focused his attention on the team. "I have some good news. We got the Fontaine mansion for the shoot. So everything is a go. Paul, I need to get with you a bit later to make a few enhancements to the agreement and then get it over to legal for a quick look."

"Sure thing, boss."

"Diane, I want to get some location shots set up and put on the schedule. When are Stacey and Norm getting in?"

"They should be landing as we speak. They took the red-eye from LA. A car is waiting for them at the airport," Diane said of the unit manager and technical director.

"Good." Craig checked his watch. "Let's all meet when Norm and Stacey arrive," he said. His glance spanned to include everyone. He turned to Anthony, clapped him on the shoulder and with a toss of his head indicated that he wanted to talk out of earshot. He led the way out and across the hall to his room.

Anthony shut the door behind them. "Lemme hear it. How did you get her to change her mind? I'm almost afraid to ask."

Craig tossed him a withering look from over his shoulder. "Yo, what are you trying to say, man?"

"I'm not *trying* to say anything. I'm saying you sometimes maneuver women into that horizontal position that magically gets them to do what you want."

"One time," he corrected, holding up his index finger as pseudoproof.

"Twice."

"All right, all right. Twice. But it was mutual. I never have a woman do anything they don't truly want to do. I'm not that guy."

"Yeah, yeah, I know, man. I'm just pulling your chain." He crossed the carpeted floor to the counter, fixed himself a cup of coffee then took a seat in a club chair by the window. "So, what's the deal?"

Craig sat on the lounge chair and stretched his long legs out in front of him, crossing his feet at the ankles. He linked his fingers across his hard belly. "I made her an offer she couldn't refuse," he said in a pretty good imitation of Marlon Brando's Vito Corleone.

"Yeah, what kind of offer?"

"Well, I was honest . . . or at least as honest as I can be. I told her exactly how important this film is to me and why. We talked." His gaze drifted away as an image of Jewel filled his line of sight. A grin curved his mouth.

"She must have said something pretty powerful to put that look on your face."

Craig blinked, gave a quick shake of his head and returned his attention to Anthony. "I don't know what it was, to be honest." He leaned forward and rested his arms on his thighs. "There's . . . something about

53

her. Can't put my finger on it." He looked Anthony right in the eyes. "Getting her to agree to let us use her home for the shoot is a major coup, no doubt, but having lunch with her tomorrow is the icing on the cake." He grinned.

"You dog," Anthony teased, wagging a finger at him.

"It's not like that," Craig said, chuckling. "I swear."

"Not yet."

"Look, I asked her to dinner, and she flat-out said no. I bumped it down to lunch with the caveat that if she agreed I would tell her why I haven't been back for ten years."

Anthony's dark eyes widened in surprise. "Say what?"

"She wanted to know . . . and that was the only thing I could offer to get her to agree to lunch."

"The offer she couldn't refuse," Anthony said.

"Yeah, something like that."

"Let me get this straight. You meet this woman. You want something from her. She tells you no — something you aren't used to hearing, by the way — and you offer to reveal to her something *I* only got out of you after years of friendship and a bottle of bourbon? Is that about right?"

"Maybe if you'd had her body, those eyes and that mouth I would have told you sooner," he joked.

Anthony burst out laughing, sputtering coffee. He grabbed a napkin and wiped his mouth then leveled his gaze at his friend. "Hey, it's cool, whatever you want to do. I'm just saying be clearheaded — that's all. In another three months, we'll be back in London for the next film. Long distance has never been your thing."

Craig pressed his lips together and slowly nodded his head. "Yeah, I know. It's all good."

"Now for the practical question, how much more is this going to cost us?"

"Another ten grand."

"What? Craig, man, we have a budget, remember? You're adding ten K to the budget and we haven't even started shooting yet."

"I got this. Don't worry." He stood.

"It's my job to worry. It's what I do. I know you have deep pockets, but don't bust a hole in them." His cell phone chirped. He pulled it out of his shirt pocket. "It's Diane. Norm and Stacey just arrived," he said.

"Cool. Give them an hour to get settled and we'll all meet over lunch. Have room service bring up whatever everyone wants."

Anthony pushed up from his seat and set his coffee cup down on the table. He turned to Craig, slung his hands into his pockets and pushed out a breath. "I know you have a lot riding on this project," he said in a low voice. "I only want to make sure that you make it to the finish line."

"I hear you, brother." He gripped Anthony's upper arm. "I've come too far to screw this up, especially over a woman. No worries. Okay?"

Anthony studied him for a moment. "See you at lunch." He turned and walked out.

Craig faced the window that offered a panorama of the place he'd once called home. He knew that Anthony was only doing his job. When he put on his other hat as first assistant director it was his responsibility to keep everything on point, including keeping an eye on the budget. But Craig also knew that wasn't Anthony's main concern. His concern rose out of their decades-long friendship. Anthony knew him, knew the demons that he dealt with — the string of relationships to fight the bouts of depression, the outbursts of anger and the weeks of isolation. The chasm between him and his father was at the center of it all, that and his very publicly failed engagement to international model and up-and-coming film star Anastasia Dumont, the daughter of Alexander Dumont, the London financier. Although the disaster of their engagement had ended three years earlier and it happened across the pond, it still stung. His and Anastasia's faces and every detail of their relationship — at least what the tabloids could piece together — became cover copy for every pop magazine here and abroad for months. At least until the next personal scandal took center stage.

He'd almost waited by the phone for a call from his father telling him, "I told you so." Craig wasn't sure what stung more, the fact that the call never came or that his father didn't even care enough to say, "I told you so."

Anthony was right. He had to keep his head on straight and not get distracted by a beautiful woman who clearly had major issues of her own. The last thing he needed was to haul around someone else's baggage. He'd tell her just enough to tamp down her curiosity, and that was it. He was as good at masking what rested behind his emotional armor as he was a writer and director — and he had the awards to prove it. Whatever he didn't want Ms. Jewel Fontaine to know she would never know.

■ ■ ■ ■

"I'm going to take your father on a stroll around the grounds," Minerva said as she walked into the sitting room off the veranda.

Jewel placed the newspaper that she was reading down on the table. "I think I'll go with you. I could use some exercise myself." She pushed up from the chair.

"I saw a car pull off earlier. Was that the film people?"

Jewel tugged on her bottom lip with her teeth before answering. "Yes. It was Mr. Lawson."

"Oh." Her voice rose in a note of surprise. "And?" she added when Jewel offered nothing further.

"He came to ask me to reconsider."

"And?"

"And I agreed." She held onto her smile.

Minerva clapped her hands together in delighted relief. "Amen! I am so happy that you came to your senses."

"I'm glad you approve."

"What made you change your mind?"

"I thought about what you said." Craig Lawson immediately came to mind. "It's for the best."

Minerva squeezed Jewel's arm. "This will

lift a big burden off your shoulders and give you some room to breathe." She hesitated a moment. "I know I've said it a dozen times, but if you're set against going back to your art, you could have a whole other career in baking. It wouldn't bring in the same level of money as your paintings and such, but . . . you love it and your customers love the magic you make."

Jewel drew in a long breath and slowly released it. "One thing at a time, Minny, okay?" A faint smile of indulgence curved her mouth. "Let's go take Dad for his walk. Then I actually do need to get into the kitchen. I have an order for three dozen red velvet cupcakes for Ms. Hatfield's daughter's sweet sixteen party."

"See, they love you," Minerva said with a grin.

Jewel slowly shook her head, tucked in her smile and followed Minerva to her father's room.

He'd been out with more women than he could count or remember. There was rarely a time in his life when a woman was not somewhere in the shadows. He adored women, loved the look of them, the way they made him feel about himself. He'd experienced the gamut of emotions for the women he'd been with, but fear was never one of them. But if he were tortured and had to confess, he would admit that he was scared as all hell about this lunch thing with Jewel Fontaine.

He didn't have a damned thing to prove to her. He wasn't trying to win her over and get her into bed. This was business. So there was no reason for the churning in his gut or the galloping of his heart.

Craig made the last turn on the road toward Jewel's home and realized as he gripped the wheel that his palms were damp. What the hell? He maneuvered the Suburban slowly down the narrow dirt lane and came to a stop at the end of it. He cut the engine. Too many scenarios of what came next raced around in his head. He pushed out a breath, opened the door and got out. No point in delaying the inevitable.

He strode toward the front door and up the three steps to the landing. He rang the bell. Moments later the nurse came to the door.

"Good afternoon, Mr. Lawson," she greeted him with a wide grin. "Ms. Fontaine is expecting you. Please come in."

All very Southern, Craig mused. "Thank you." He stepped inside and was once again taken aback by the sweeping grandeur of the home. Tastefully elegant in every detail.

"You can have a seat in the parlor." She indicated the room to her right with a tilt of her hand. "I'll let Ms. Fontaine know that you're here. Can I get you anything?" she asked before turning away.

"No, thank you, ma'am. I'm fine."

Minerva hurried off.

Craig took a slow turn in the well-appointed room. Old-world charm seeped from every corner. The oak beams, padded antique chairs, heavy glass and wood tables and gleaming hardwood floors with strategically placed area carpeting all added to the flavor of what once was and still existed. He could envision the cigar smoke drifting into the air while men of power sat around making decisions and sipping shots of whiskey.

"Sorry to keep you waiting."

Craig turned toward the sound of Jewel's voice and was hit once again with the impact of seeing her. He swallowed. His lips parted for a moment before a response could form.

"Not a problem," he finally said. He took a step toward her. Her eyes widened, and her bottom lip quivered ever so slightly. What was she thinking? If only he could let her know how hard it was for him to rein in the overwhelming desire to kick the door closed, press her body against the wall and kiss away the shimmering gloss she had on those lush lips. He shoved his hands into his pockets to hide the rise that pulsed and to keep from touching her. That would be a mistake. He tipped his head slightly to the side. "Ready?"

"Yes." She spun away and led the way out, giving Craig ample time to pull himself together — although looking at her from the rear wasn't much help, either.

They stepped out into the balmy early afternoon. The sky was crystal clear, the sun high and strong with a breeze off the surrounding brooks and streams cooling the air and carrying the scent of the spring blooms that sprouted from the ground and hung from the trees.

"Did you have someplace in mind?" Jewel asked while Craig held the passenger door for her and helped her in.

"Um, not really," he drawled. He shut the door and rounded the vehicle then slid in behind the wheel. He turned to look at her. "I was hoping you would suggest your favorite place," he tossed out as a Hail Mary.

Jewel grinned. "To be honest, it's been a minute since I've been out. Can't really say I have a favorite place."

Craig turned the key in the ignition.

"Then we'll find a favorite place together. Sound like a plan?"

Jewel fastened her seat belt. "Sure. Let's go."

"I'm working off rusty memory," Craig said as he pulled onto the main road. "From what I remember there are a bunch of cafés and restaurants downtown. Right?"

"Good memory. I can't guarantee they're exactly what you remember, though. There's been a lot of turnover of small businesses the past few years."

"Hmm, I can imagine. It's always the little guy that gets hit the hardest when change comes."

"Unfortunate and true."

Craig stole a look and caught the pensive expression that drew her tapered brows together. "Anyone you know?" he gently asked.

Jewel considered the question for a moment. She nodded. "Phyllis Heywood. She owned a small boutique with a lot of handmade jewelry and accessories. The rent got so high she couldn't keep the place. Then there's the bookstore and the diner that were around since I was a girl." She paused. "They've all been replaced with high-end shops and a real estate office. And those are the ones that I know about."

"Ouch."

"Exactly. And of course there are the businesses that never recovered after Katrina. A lot of people are still living in trailers and are out of work."

Craig nodded. "I know it won't solve all the problems that are going on down here, but this film will definitely bring business and jobs to the community."

"But for how long?"

He wasn't ready to reveal his entire plan. There was no guarantee that it would all pan out. "Let's say we'll take it one day at a time." He reached over and covered her hand with his. An electric charge shot between them.

Jewel's eyes seemed to brighten, and Craig heard her short intake of breath that matched his own. If he was going to get through this business lunch in one piece and not find some hidden corner to ravish her in, he was going to have to keep his hands to himself. He returned both hands to the wheel and concentrated on the winding road.

Once they were in the center of town, Craig suggested that he find a place to park and they walk around until they settled on a place to eat.

They strolled along the streets of downtown New Orleans and shared comments on the many changes that had engulfed the area. Intermittently their arms or fingertips brushed as they sidestepped other walkers and pretended the subtle touches didn't happen. Instinctively, Craig's hand found its way to the center of her lower back as he guided her along the narrow streets. The heat from her body sizzled on his fingertips, and it took all of his concentration to stay on task and not focus on what her skin would feel like next to his. *Talk, don't think,* he reminded himself. *Talk.*

"I know it's been a while since I've been here, but I got to admit, it feels totally different. Nothing like I remembered," he said. "I mean, it kind of looks the same, but the vibe is off."

"I know what you mean. I feel the same way. The only difference is that I've been here to see it happen."

"Hmm." He lifted his chin in the direction of a small bistro up ahead with a sandwich board out front announcing its menu. "Let's check this place out."

They walked up to the sandwich board, scanned the menu, looked at each other and grinned in agreement. Craig held the door open for her, and they stepped inside.

The interior of Appetite Noir took one back to the early days of good old down-home New Orleans eating. The heavy wood beams, picnic-style tables, stained wood floors, zydeco and blues in the background, and the aromas of barbecue and crayfish made a tantalizing combination.

"Table for two?" a young hostess asked.

"Yes, please," Craig responded.

The waitress grabbed two menus and instructed them to follow her. Craig took the opportunity to drop his hand to the small of Jewel's back once again, and the gesture was still as thrilling.

The waitress stopped in front of a small booth-type seating arrangement and placed the menus on the table. "Your server will be right with you. Enjoy."

"I didn't even know this place was here," Jewel said as she took a slow look around. She set her purse on the space next to her and lifted her menu. Sitting opposite Craig Lawson would take work on her part. She would have to pretend that his eyes didn't affect her, that they didn't have the power to strip her of her facade. She would have to avoid watching his lips move when he spoke so that she wouldn't fantasize about how they would feel, what he would taste like.

She stared at the menu. The words swirled around in front of her. This was why she should have said no. Stirring up the dead embers of her soul could serve no purpose other than to lead her down a road of momentary fantasy. To even imagine that there could be something between them was silly, childish. Craig Lawson was a man of the world. A womanizing man of the world based on what she'd read on the internet. He was a man that cast his lot into a world of make-believe. He'd left his home, his family, his roots to run after a dream. And there didn't seem to be anyone or anything that had slowed him in that pursuit. But what would it be like to become part of the fantasy — even for a little while?

"Know what you want?"

Jewel blinked. Her gaze landed on his face, and she was certain he could read the salacious thoughts she'd had about him. She swallowed. "Um, no. Everything looks good."

Craig chuckled. "That is true. But I can't remember when I last had some Nawlins crayfish. I want a bucketful."

Jewel laughed. "Me, too, now that I think about it."

Craig slapped his palms on the table and leaned forward. "You gotta be kidding me. You're right here in the mix."

He tipped his head back in disbelief, and Jewel stole a quick look at the tight cords of his neck. She ran her tongue across her lips. "Guilty," she murmured.

Craig's gaze settled on her face. "We 'bout to change that right now, darlin'." His right brow rose to punctuate his declaration just as their waitress approached.

They placed their order for two buckets of crayfish, seasoned fries, coleslaw and a pitcher of beer.

"I'm going to regret this in the morning," Jewel said when the humongous order arrived and was placed in front of them.

"Live for the moment, darlin'. Sometimes we just have to give in to our fantasies."

Jewel's belly clenched. It was as if he'd read her mind or channeled her thoughts. She cleared her throat. "Maybe you're right."

For the next few minutes, the only conversation between them was groans of delight.

"Damn, I missed this," Craig finally said. He wiped his fingers and mouth with the linen napkin and then took a long swallow of beer. The bucket was still half-full.

Jewel wiped her fingers and mouth as well

and pushed out a breath. "Whew." She giggled. "I haven't thrown down like that for a while." She put her napkin aside. "So, Mr. Lawson, I hope you don't think that I've forgotten our agreement." She reached for her mug of beer.

"Agreement? The film?"

She pursed her lips in feigned annoyance. "You know perfectly well that's not what I mean."

He tried to look sheepish. "Okay, fine. What do you want to know?"

"If you missed this all so much," she said with an encompassing wave of her hands, "then why did you stay away for so long?"

Craig linked his long fingers together, rocked his jaw and took a sobering breath. "I'm sure you've heard about my family — the famous and the infamous." He chuckled.

"A little — more about your uncle the senator."

Craig nodded. "Well, there is a whole host of us Lawsons. And from birth expectation is high — unreachable for some of us. We had to live up to the long legacy of the name as well as what was deemed to be our role in the ongoing saga of our lives."

"And you clearly decided that you weren't going to toe the family line."

He snorted a laugh. "Something like that. It didn't go over well."

"What was it that you didn't want to do?"

Craig paused, trying to frame the story in his head. "My father, Jake Lawson, is the youngest of the three brothers. My uncle Paul is the eldest, and my uncle Branford the senator. My grandfather Clive runs the family — his sons — like a well-oiled machine. He set down the template for success, and none of his sons ever deviated from it. Gramps's grandparents were slaves. His parents grew up on a plantation." His gaze rose from studying his fingers to land on her face. "Very much like your home." He took another swallow of his beer. "My template was to follow in my father's footsteps. Jake Lawson is probably — at least the last time I checked — the most influential land developer in the country. If it's being bought, sold or imagined, my father more than likely has a hand in it."

"And he wanted you to join the family business."

Craig nodded in agreement. "It wasn't for me."

"Why wouldn't your father want his son to pursue his own destiny?"

His jaw clenched. He glanced away. "He has his reasons," he said, his voice low and gravelly.

Jewel watched the array of emotions flit across Craig's countenance. There was clearly more there than he was telling. But it wasn't her place to pull it out of him. Everyone was entitled to their secrets, her included.

"You have sisters and brothers?" she asked, attempting to lift him out of the pit that he'd lowered himself into.

A soft smile tugged at the corners of his mouth. "Yeah, my brother, Myles, and my sister, Alyse."

"Do they live here?"

"Yeah."

"They must miss you," she said softly. As an only child, she'd never known what it felt like to have a sibling to share a life with, memories, joys and sorrows.

Craig finished off his beer, peeled the shell off a crayfish and popped it in his mouth. He chewed slowly. "You have sisters and brothers?" he asked, changing the subject.

"No. Just me."

They studied each other for a moment.

"What did your parents want for you?"

Her expression softened. "They wanted me to be happy. My happiness took the form of art, and my dad was behind me a thousand percent."

"What about your mom?"

Her deep sigh was audible. "She died when I was six. Ovarian cancer."

"Oh . . . man, I'm really sorry."

"It's okay." She swallowed. "My dad . . . he really stepped up. He was mom, dad and my best friend. He sacrificed a lot so that I could pursue my art. I'll never be able to repay him for all that he did for me." She expelled a breath as a wave of sadness swept through her. She pushed it away. "So what do you do besides create make-believe and date all your leading ladies?"

Craig tossed his head back and let loose a hearty laugh that warmed Jewel all the way down to her toes. It was a feel-good laugh.

"Ah, Ms. Fontaine, you wound me," he said in an exaggerated drawl. He pressed his hand to his chest.

"Well, if it's on the internet, it must be true," she teased.

"Yeah, right. And Kanye will win as president."

"Touché." But she really *did* want him to tell her about the women in his life. Did they matter? Did he remember their names? Would he remember hers?

He leaned back in his seat and angled his head to the side. "The tabloids, TMZ . . . always blow things out of proportion. They always think they have the inside story on what goes on in people's private lives."

His voice had taken on a hard edge, Jewel realized.

"They don't. They have no clue and what they don't know they make up." He refilled his beer mug from the pitcher.

"Is that what happened to you?" she asked softly.

His dark eyes flashed for a moment, and in that split second she caught the depth of hurt that swam beneath, and then just as quickly it was gone.

Craig shrugged. "It comes with the territory, darlin'." A smile curved his mouth. He lifted his mug and took a short swallow of beer.

"Do you watch your own films?" Jewel asked with a warm smile. She knew that they needed to switch gears, lighten the mood and move away from the murky waters of the past.

Craig grinned. "Only the dailies."

"Dailies?"

"Yeah. The cuts from each day of shooting." He rested his arms on the table and launched into an animated discussion about the behind-the-scenes activities of filmmaking.

Jewel listened, fascinated as much by what

she learned about the moviemaking process as what she did about Craig Lawson. He was a passionate man. A dedicated man, a man of conviction. He respected his crew and was loyal to his friends. Like her he was well traveled, and much to her amazement he spoke French and Spanish — just as she did. He told her about some of his many trips around the globe, the people that he'd met, the customs and cultures that he'd encountered. Like his uncle Branford, he was well versed in the political climate of the States as well as abroad. And nowhere in any of the scenarios that he presented was there a significant other in the picture.

"Can I get you two anything else?"

They both looked up at the server that they didn't recognize then took a look around the restaurant. The clientele had shifted from late lunch goers to dinner guests — they could tell by the briefcases resting beside polished shoes and the relief in the after-work laughter. They'd been talking for hours.

Craig grinned at Jewel. "Uh, I think we're done. Can I get the check, please?"

"Sure thing." She slipped the leather carrier out of her apron pocket and placed it on the table.

The instant she turned away, Jewel and

Craig burst into laughter. Jewel checked her watch. "We've been here for almost four hours!"

"Time flies when you're in good company," he said as his gaze settled slowly and completely on her face.

Jewel felt the heat rise to her cheeks. Her stomach fluttered. "Yes, it does," she said softly.

They strolled slowly back to Craig's vehicle, commenting on the shops and people that they passed along the way.

This felt good, Jewel realized. It had been so long that she'd been out with a man she'd forgotten how wonderful it felt to be looked after, admired, to be in the company of a handsome, sexy man that any woman would switch places with her to be with. But this was real life, not some story on the big screen. She knew in her gut that nothing much could happen between them. In another couple of months he'd be gone, on to his next project in some far-flung corner of the world.

She studied his profile as they walked and talked. It was as if his features had been carved by a skilled hand. She wanted to reach out and stroke the curve of his jaw, the angle of his forehead, run her finger along the full lips. And then as if he was once again reading her thoughts, he took her hand. The jolt of the contact set her heart racing.

His long fingers curved around her hand and held it possessively. She stared at him. He brought her hand to his lips and tenderly kissed it then continued walking, as if they always walked through the streets of downtown New Orleans holding hands.

"Thank you for a lovely afternoon," Craig said with a smoldering smile.

They stood facing each other, inches apart, on her front porch. Jewel's heart thumped. "I'm glad I went."

"Are you?" His brows tightened as he took a step closer, forcing her to look up.

Her throat worked. "Very."

"That's good to know, because I want to do it again."

Jewel swallowed. "Lunch?"

"Dinner . . . and then breakfast."

The implication was clear. Heat flashed through her limbs. Her head swam.

"How does that sound?"

"It sounds : . ."

Before she could form the words, he'd slid his arm around her waist and pulled her flush against the hard lines of his body, and the world disappeared as his head came down and those lips that she had fantasized about kissing covered hers. The kiss was electric, slow and sweet. She couldn't think over the hum that echoed deep in his throat as he deepened their kiss, teasing her mouth with a swipe of his tongue. Her entire body vibrated and felt weak all at once. Her fingers held onto the tight ropes of his arms, and all she could piece together in her head was that she didn't want it to end. But then it did.

Craig looked down into her upturned face. "You let me know when," he said, his voice low and ragged. He traced her bottom lip with the tip of his finger, turned and strode down the walkway to his car, and like waking from a dream he was gone.

But it wasn't a dream. She ran her tongue across her lips and tasted him, shut her eyes and saw him. It was very real.

CHAPTER 4

Craig was met at the front door of the hotel by the black-jacketed valet that gallantly opened the chrome and glass door and wished him a practiced "Enjoy your stay." Craig strode across the lobby floor and stabbed the up button on the elevator panel. He was more than two hours late for his sit-down with his team. He hadn't intended to be gone as long as he had, and neither had he intended to be so affected by a simple kiss. The entire ride back from Jewel's home to the hotel his thoughts leapfrogged each other, never allowing him a moment to catch them and try to figure out what he was thinking and feeling.

"Well, there you are," Anthony greeted him the moment Craig entered the suite. "Thought you'd forgotten all about us." He eyed Craig for a response.

"Yeah, sorry for the delay. Got caught up." He avoided Anthony's pointed stare and

78

shrugged out of his lightweight leather jacket and tossed it on a chair. "Where are we with things?"

"Everyone has arrived, and we were working out the shooting schedule. The primary actors, Milan and Hamilton, arrived about an hour ago. They're getting settled in their rooms."

Craig nodded, taking in the information. "Cool. I want to have a sit-down with the primaries in about an hour."

"Sure." He paused. "So . . . how was lunch?"

"Filling." His cell phone chirped in his pocket. He pulled it out and saw his sister's name on the screen. He blew out a breath. "Gotta take this." He pressed the talk icon. "Hey, sis." He turned away from Anthony and crossed the room to the window. "How are you?" He didn't have to wait long for his sister to read him the riot act.

"Why do I have to read about you being back in town? You couldn't call?"

Craig briefly shut his eyes. He knew his sister. And when she went on a tear, she didn't stop until she was beyond satisfied. "Sorry, sis. I've been crazy busy from the moment we landed."

"Lousy excuse," she groused. "So," she puffed into the phone. "How are you and where are you staying?"

He held back a smile, envisioning his petite sister's dark eyes cinched at the corners and her mouth in a tight, disapproving line. As the youngest of the three and the only girl, Alyse learned early that she had to be just as tough if not tougher than her big brothers and be able to stand toe to toe with their father.

"I'm fine, thanks, sis. And I'm staying at the Marriott in the Quarter."

"Fancy," she teased. "So I'm free this evening. I can meet you at your hotel."

Craig knew that, much like him, the word *no* didn't factor into Alyse's vocabulary. He exhaled slowly. "Sure. How about eight?"

"I'll see you then. Myles is out of town, by the way. But he should be back by the weekend."

"I'll be sure to give him a call."

The elephant sat between them. Their father. Thankfully Alyse didn't bring him up. Craig was not in the mood to discuss their father at the moment, but he knew he wouldn't be able to avoid the conversation later. "Look, sis, I gotta run. I'll see you tonight."

"Fine. Looking forward to seeing you, Craig," she said, her tone finally softening.

"Me, too, sis. Later." He disconnected the

call, shook his head and slid the phone back into his pocket. The sound of voices and activity drew his attention to the main room. Milan Chase had arrived, and one would think that his crew had never been in the presence of a movie star with the way they tripped over each other to introduce themselves.

Milan Chase was the epitome of classy, sexy beauty, but more than that she was an incredible actress who knew her worth down to the last penny and who had two Golden Globes and an Oscar nomination to her credit. Not only was she good at what she did on camera, she was an astute businesswoman who was notorious for tough negotiations for all of her contracts. Even her lawyers deferred to her. He'd had brief reservations in casting Milan for the lead role. Not because of her ability, but because of their history.

Craig entered the open living space, and like the parting of the sea, his crew moved aside as he strode toward Milan.

"Glad you got here safe and sound," he said in an intimate tone. He took her hands in his and kissed her right cheek then her left.

"Craig," she said in her patented throaty whisper. "Good to see you again." Her

81

lashes fluttered for an instant.

"You, too. How are your accommodations?"

"Perfect."

"Good." He released her hands. "I was in the midst of planning a meeting in about an hour. You good with that?" He slung his hands into his pockets.

"Absolutely. I'm anxious to get started."

Craig nodded. "You can hang out here or wait in your room until we're ready. Up to you."

"I might as well stay, get familiar with the crew."

"That's fine." He patted her shoulder and started to move away.

"Craig . . ."

He glanced over his shoulder then turned. "Yeah?"

Milan stepped closer. "Are you free later tonight?"

His eyes widened for an instant. "Tonight? Actually, I have plans."

She lowered her gaze then looked directly at him. "Tomorrow night, then."

He cleared his throat. "I'll, uh, let you know. Is there a problem?"

"Not at all. I thought we could catch up for old times' sake."

He rocked his jaw. The last thing he

needed was to rekindle the embers with Milan, but he didn't want her as an adversary, either. "Maybe we can do drinks," he offered to appease her. "How's that?"

"Sure." She flashed her movie star smile. "Drinks sound fine."

"Craig . . ."

He turned toward the sound of his name. "Duty calls. Check you later." He walked over to Anthony.

"Yeah, what's up?"

"Looked like you needed rescuing," Anthony said under his breath.

"You noticed that, huh? Thanks."

"I let everyone know to be in place for the meeting. The main thing is the shooting schedule for week one. Everything cool with the location?"

"Yes. I have some adjustments to make to the contract and I'll get it signed."

Anthony's right brow rose. "You? Paul or Diane can do that."

"I'd prefer to handle it myself."

"Mmm-hmm."

"Don't, okay? It's not like that."

"Hey, my man. It's your party. All I ask is to keep the fireworks to a minimum."

Craig slapped Anthony's back. "No worries." He caught a glimpse of Milan out of the corner of his eye. He hoped that sentiment would remain true. "Got a call from Alyse."

"You knew that was going to happen."

He snorted a laugh. "Yeah. Meeting her later tonight at the hotel bar."

"Public place. Good move," he teased.

"Very funny."

"Well, you know how Alyse can be."

"That I do," he conceded good-naturedly. He pushed out a breath. "Soon as Hamilton gets here, we can get started."

"In the meantime, let's go over a few things for the shooting schedule and the staffing."

"Sure."

"So what about your pops?" Anthony hedged once they were seated at the round table away from the team.

Craig looked up from the notes on the iPad. "What about him?"

"Guess that answers my question."

"I hope so."

Jewel finished packing up the bakery boxes filled with cupcakes for her client's daughter's sixteenth-birthday party. She tied each box with her signature lavender bow and tucked a business card in each one. She had to admit that over the past few months the requests for her baking services had increased considerably. As it currently stood, she had the space in her kitchen and the time on her hands to efficiently complete her orders. But she wasn't too sure how long that efficiency would last at this rate. The extra income wasn't enough for her to sit back and relax, but it did help. Maybe Minerva was right and this was her next career move, which shifted her thoughts back to her lunch and conversation with Craig. It was exhilarating and simultaneously disheartening to listen to his unwavering passion for his work. She'd had that once. And had anyone asked her five years earlier if she ever saw anything different in her life, she would have responded with a flat-out no.

The past five years had been hard, harder than she often admitted even in the quiet of her own mind. There were those days when she missed the travel, the work, the accolades, the excitement of creating something from nothing, allowing her imagination to become a physical reality.

There were times when she'd questioned her decision to leave that life behind her, to throw in the towel, so to speak. Yet, even after all this time, her fall from grace still stung.

It was a New York showing. The promotion leading up to her gallery opening had been in every art magazine, newspaper and blog and on the lips of every reputable critic in the business. The buzz in the art world was near deafening in anticipation of Jewel Fontaine's new work. Rumor had it that she had taken a departure from her traditional oil painting and classic sculptures to something more avant-garde and edgy. It was a risk. But the artistic visionary in her guided her in a new direction.

She'd always been anxious on opening nights, but this night was different. She was actually scared. Her personal assistant, Mai Ling, had spent the better part of the day convincing her that the fans and the critics would love it.

"You're a brilliant artist, Jewel," Mai said. "You've carved a solid reputation for excellence, and one show is not going to change that. The work is phenomenal, and anyone with a grain of sense will see it. So stop worrying. It's going to be fine." She gave Jewel a reassuring hug. "I put your outfit on the bed. The car will be here to pick us up at six. You have an interview with *Art Digest* and the reviewer from the *Times*. Then it's on to the after-party."

Jewel pushed out a breath. She didn't know what she would do without Mai. *Ef-*

ficient wasn't a word that did her justice. "Great. And you have the car to pick up my father from the airport?"

"Of course. I don't want you to worry about anything beyond looking beautiful and talking about your work."

"I'll try. Is Simon coming?" she asked with an edge of doubt in her voice.

Mai's lashes fanned her eyes. "He didn't RSVP," she said softly. "But you know Simon. He never was one to follow protocol."

Jewel knew that Mai was attempting to ease her angst, but the truth was her on-again, off-again relationship with Simon Devareau had been switched to the off mode for weeks. Simon was a writer and arranger for some of the biggest names in the music industry, and his time and talent were always in demand. He was a temperamental musical genius who could go for weeks, sometimes months without seeing or talking to her when he was in the throes of composing new work.

They'd met on the beaches of Rio two years earlier and had hit if off almost instantly. She was magnetically drawn to his brooding good looks and his passion for his work. They shared many things in common, the arts being one and mind-blowing sex the other. They spent endless hours discussing their work, sharing ideas, sparking others. But Simon always maintained an invisible wall, one that she was never able to penetrate. She wanted more. He knew it, and the wall grew thicker and higher. Their times apart became longer, the silences louder. Jewel wanted it to work. She believed that there was room in their lives for each other and the work. Simon didn't say it in so many words, but his actions spoke volumes — his work took priority. Period. And the harder she tried to make him cross the line, the harder he pulled away. She knew it was a mistake to hope that he would be there for her big night, but she couldn't stamp out her need to want him with her.

"I'm going to head over to the Guggenheim and make sure that there are no last-minute glitches, then I'll meet you back here no later than five so that I can get ready."

"Thanks, sweetie. Call me if there are any problems."

Mai gave her an *are you kidding me* look, shook her head and walked out.

When the limo pulled up in front of the Guggenheim Museum, it was a scene right out of Oscar night. The red carpet led from the street up to the front entrance to the museum. Reporters and photographers lined the roped-off entrance, and the instant Jewel stepped from the limo behind Mai, the flash of lights from cameras and cell phones and the shouting of her name rose in a cacophony of light and sound. The reception was overwhelming, and Jewel's stress level skyrocketed. She did her best to keep her smile in place as she walked the carpet, stopping every several feet to take a picture or answer a quick question. Finally they made it inside.

The Ronald O. Perelman Rotunda designed by the iconic Frank Lloyd Wright could hold fourteen hundred people for a reception and three hundred for a sit-down dinner. Even Jewel gasped at the opulence of the space that was strategically lined with her latest work, set off by the polished glass and chrome of the event space and marble floors. Circular linen-topped tables with white votive candles as centerpieces were arranged to the side of the space to accommodate the after-party dinner reception.

"Oh. My. God," Jewel said in a gush of awe.

Mai squeezed Jewel's bare arm. "It's going to be a fabulous night," she whispered in assurance. "Now let's mingle." Mai took Jewel's arm and guided her around the extraordinary space.

If only Mai's prediction had been true. It was apparent within the first hour that the buzz among the patrons and the press was anything but complimentary.

"Terrible."

"Not her style."

"What happened to her?"

"Definitely not what I expected."

"Disappointing."

Jewel tried hard to ignore the demoralizing commentary. But the sit-down dinner where she was surrounded by self-declared connoisseurs of art who worked hard at maintaining polite conversation that pointedly didn't include the exhibit, was the longest night of her life, with the only highlight being that Simon did arrive and was by her side during the interminable meal.

There were points when she wanted to run out and break down and cry, but she knew she had to keep up the front of confidence.

The silence was so heavy on the ride back to her hotel that it made her head pound. Simon offered to spend the night, and for the first time since they'd been a couple she turned him down. She needed to be alone and didn't want him to be around when she read the reviews in the morning. The fact that her father was a witness to her embarrassment was enough.

She sat opposite Mai the following morning looking at one review after another that eviscerated her work. Every outlet from the venerable *New York Times* to *New York* magazine, *Art and Culture, Contemporary Art Review* and every blog and newspaper in between were, uncharacteristically, in agreement — the exhibit was an epic failure. Even the international press had a field day at her expense. One critic went so far as to intimate that Jewel Fontaine's star had finally fallen.

"Jewel . . . I am so sorry. I don't know what to say."

Jewel lifted the coffee mug to her lips and took a sip. "There's nothing to say. It's all here," she said, pushing the papers aside. She glanced off into the distance.

"You know how critics are. They wouldn't be critics if they didn't have something to disparage. It will pass. All of the great artists were blasted by detractors that didn't understand what the artist was trying to convey."

"Not like this." She huffed. "Some of these reviews are almost personal."

"But you can't take it personally."

"I know you're trying to make me feel better, Mai. You're wasting your time." Jewel pushed away from the table and stood. "I'm going to get dressed, pack my bags, meet my father and go back home."

"The flight is at one."

"Hmm. Thanks."

The trip back home with her father was the second and ultimate blow.

For the prior six months Jewel had been traveling, studying and immersing herself in the production for her show at the Guggenheim. She kept in contact with her father by phone. They spoke at least once per week. The small lapses in the conversation, the long pauses between one idea and the next, and often the disassociation with whatever it was that they were discussing she tossed off as her father, much like herself, being preoccupied. When she saw him for the first time in six months, he physically looked the same, but there was often a vacancy in his eyes and a faraway tone in his voice. This she attributed to the travel, exhaustion and the excitement of the evening. The plane ride, however, was the most devastating experience of her life.

One moment her father seemed perfectly fine. Then he began referring to Jewel by her mother's name — Estelle — and by degrees he became more and more agitated and seemingly disoriented, not understanding why he was on a plane or where he was going. Jewel was terrified, and his agitation grew to a point where the flight attendants had to intervene. Fortunately they were only twenty minutes out of Louisiana and Jewel was able to calm him without him being restrained. By the time they landed, he seemed to be himself again, but exhausted, as if the lapse had been as much physical as mental.

The diagnosis was what every child fears for their parent — early-onset Alzheimer's disease. Whatever idea Jewel might have had about returning to New York or going back to Europe came to a grinding halt. Her father couldn't be left alone, especially in that enormous house. The doctors prescribed the latest in medication that was touted to slow the disease but not stop it. For a while the medication seemed to work, and then it didn't. They tried combination after combination, with the same result — "You should put him a facility where he can be cared for." For Jewel that was not an option.

Augustus Fontaine was her dad. The man who had been her rock for the better part of her life. Now it was her turn to be there for him.

For a while she tried to paint, to sculpt, but her father needed her more and more. Maybe it was some macabre blessing in disguise, she often thought. After the debacle of her showing at the Guggenheim, no one was beating down her door. She'd lost her mojo, and there seemed to be nowhere in her day or in her life for her to reclaim it. Instead, she turned all of her time and attention to caring for her father, until it became too much for her to handle alone. She hired Minerva.

That had been a little more than two years ago. The disease had plateaued and remained at the same stage for quite some time. She supposed that was a good thing, and she'd fully accepted the turn that her life had taken. But the hard reality of her father's care had done major damage to her bank account, and without the income from sales of her work, tours and speaking engagements, there was not much to replenish it with.

And then came Craig Lawson.

"Need any help with those?" Minerva walked into the kitchen and settled on the opposite side of the counter.

"I'm almost done. Thanks. How's Dad?"

"Fine. He had a good day. And might I ask about yours?"

Jewel tucked in a grin and busied herself with stacking the boxes. "Well . . . it was very nice."

"How nice?" she probed.

Jewel pushed out a breath. "Nice enough that I might do it again . . . if he asks."

Minerva's light brown eyes widened. She clapped her hands in delight. "Hallelujah, and let the choir say amen!"

Jewel couldn't help but laugh. "Gee whiz, Minerva, it's not that bad."

"Oh, yes, it is. When was the last time you went out . . . with a man?" There was a long pause. "Exactly. And it don't hurt that he's drop-dead gorgeous and wealthy."

"That's all very true, but you are getting way ahead of what is going on. He lives between London and California. He has the kind of life that I have been out of for quite some time. Even if there was something going on between us — which there isn't — there would be no way to make it work," she added dismissively, even as she replayed the way his mouth felt on hers, the way he tasted and the way she wanted more. "It's just two adults in a business arrangement that somewhat enjoy each other's company."

"Hmm," Minerva murmured with a rise

in her brow. "If you say so." She started for the archway that led to the dining room. "I have to run into town to pick up a few things. I should be back in an hour or so. Do you need anything?"

"No. I'm good. I'm going to sit with Dad for a while."

"Okay. See you soon."

Jewel plopped down on the stool and gazed off into the distance, trying to paint a portrait of what her life might look like with a man like Craig Lawson in it. But then she looked at the stack of bakery boxes and her eyes lifted to the floor above where her father slept. She pushed back from her seat and stood. This was her life.

Throughout the meeting with his team, Craig struggled with keeping focused on the items at hand. His thoughts continually shifted between topics of discussion and kissing Jewel Fontaine. He was pretty sure that was a bad move on his part. He had a long history of getting involved with people he worked with, Milan Chase being a prime example. He didn't want his somewhat jaded history to repeat itself with Jewel, but the truth of the matter was that, as inappropriate as it might be, he wanted to see her again. He wanted to take her to his bed and strip her naked. He needed to see and feel for himself if her skin was as silken as it looked. Did that lovely scent that drifted around her find its way beneath those gauzy dresses she wore? What would it feel like to be sheathed inside her? The merry-go-round of his questions was endless. He was immensely happy when the meeting came to an end.

"We can start preliminary shooting next week. Exteriors," Diane was saying as Craig pushed back from the table.

"Get the full schedule printed up and sent to everyone's tablets," Craig instructed her and Paul. "Norm, you can get some stills as well for the storyboards."

"No problem, boss," Norm, the technical director, said.

Craig checked his watch. He had time to shower and change before meeting up with his sister. He crossed over to Anthony before he headed to his room. "As soon as the revised contract is ready, let me know. I'll drop it off and get it signed."

Anthony shot him a sidelong look. "Not a problem."

He walked over to the minibar and poured himself a short glass of bourbon. "I'm gonna get ready to meet up with Alyse. I need all the fortitude I can get." He tossed the warm liquid down in one swallow, shut his eyes briefly against the burn then set the glass down. He clapped Anthony on the back. "Thanks for holding it down, man."

"We got this," he said with a grin.

Craig turned away and lifted his hand in salute.

He changed into a black cotton shirt and black slacks, slid his phone, credit card and room key into his pocket, and headed down to the lobby to meet his sister.

He was seated in one of the lounge chairs checking out the day's headlines when Alyse pushed through the revolving door. She didn't see him at first, and it gave Craig the opportunity to take in and appreciate the attractive and self-assured woman his little sister had become. His heart filled with warmth and good memories, which at the same time partnered with sadness that he could have allowed his rift with his father to keep him away from his sister. He stood just as she turned her head in his direction.

Her arms stretched wide, and her dimpled smile beamed as she literally ran to him. Craig swept her up in a hug, pressing her face to his chest. She locked her arms around his waist and craned her neck to look up at him.

"God, it's so good to see you," she said as

tears formed in her eyes. She sniffed hard and stroked his strong jaw. "Those pictures are much better looking than you, though," she teased, deadpan.

Craig tossed his head back and laughed. It *would* be his little sister that had no problem giving him a reality check to remind him that he wasn't all that special. He pressed his palm to his chest. "You wound me. No respect for your elders." He grinned down at her. "It's good to see you, too, sis," he said with affection.

"Point me to the drinks and food and let's get this reunion started."

"We can go someplace else if you want," he offered.

"No, why bother? We're already here."

"Sounds good to me." Craig bent his arm and she slid hers through before leading her into the hotel's bar and restaurant.

Alyse had barely taken a breath once they were seated before she launched into her barrage of questions.

"So how long are you in town for and why didn't you tell anyone that you were coming?" She reached for her glass of water.

Craig leaned back in his seat. "About two months if everything goes according to schedule. And I know I should have called you and Myles." He paused. "I'm sorry."

"You should be. We haven't seen you in God knows how long," she groused. She shot him a glare. "I read that Milan is the lead." Her brow arched. "Ulterior motive?"

He pushed out a breath. Alyse was one of the few people other than Anthony who had told him from the start that getting involved with Milan Chase was a mistake. At the time he didn't care. They were hot for each other and they let it burn until there was nothing left but ashes.

"I don't have an ulterior motive, *and,*" he qualified, "there is nothing going on now. She happened to be the best person for the role."

"Hmm." She rolled her eyes. "Just be careful, that's all I have to say about it. But speaking about your notorious love life, who are you seeing these days?"

His thought immediately leaped to Jewel. But he couldn't truthfully count her as someone he was seeing. Besides, the minute he let Alyse know that Jewel was the owner of the location where the film was to be shot, he would never hear the end of it. "You'll be happy — or at least surprised — to know that I'm not seeing anyone. I'm totally focused on this film."

"What are your plans when it's completed?" she asked with a hint of hesitation mixed with an unspoken plea.

Craig linked his long fingers together and shrugged slightly. "When it's done I'll head back to LA, to the studio for editing, then home to London. I have a television pilot that I'm contracted to work on in the fall."

Her long lashes lowered over her eyes. "Oh," she said softly.

"But I promise to stay in touch."

The waitress came to take their drink and dinner order. Once she was gone, Alyse continued her inquisition.

"Is it true that the movie is about our family?"

Craig rocked his jaw. "Let's just say that the Lawson legacy is the inspiration for the film."

"Does Dad know?" She stared across at him.

"I have no idea what he knows. I'm sure he doesn't care one way or the other what I do," he snapped, his expression hardening by degrees.

"You don't believe that."

"Why wouldn't I? He made himself very clear, Alyse. And if nothing else, I take Jake Lawson at his word."

The last confrontation with his father still stung all these years later. As the eldest son, it was expected that he would follow in his father's footsteps and one day take over the helm of JL International. Craig had had his sights set elsewhere. Since he was a kid he'd been fascinated by the wonder and magic of film. He would watch his mother prepare for her small film roles, and sometimes she would let him come on set. His mother nurtured his thirst for the arts, his father starved him. Things only grew worse between him and his father after the scandal and his mother's tragic death. When Craig entered college, his goal was to major in film as much for himself as well as homage to his mother. His father went ballistic and refused to cover the cost unless he switched his major to international business, which he claimed to do to satisfy his father. But unknown to Jake, Craig stayed on the film track. Instead of his college graduation being a day of celebration, it was an epic nightmare when Craig's degree was an MFA in film instead of an MBA in international business.

"I don't give a damn what it was you thought you wanted! You spent my money on this piece of crap degree to do what — become famous like your trifling, lying mother!"

"Don't you dare talk about my mother!"

Jake had whirled toward his son, his face twisted in rage. He'd pointed a warning finger at Craig. "I told you —" his voice shook "— this movie shit is nothing but an empty path filled with narcissistic assholes that want gratification from everyone but themselves. It's crap. It's frivolous, and it's not worthy of a Lawson! Didn't you learn anything from what your mother did to me, to us, to this family?"

"I can't live my life for you, Dad. I can't and I won't. This is my life, my dream. You had yours. You *have* to let me have mine."

"I don't have to do a damn thing." He'd snorted a nasty laugh. His dark eyes narrowed as he glared at his son. "This is what you want. Fine." He tossed his hands up in the air as if he'd conceded defeat, but Craig instantly knew better. His father never gave in, but he'd never expected what his father said next.

Jake had pursed his lips and slid his large hands into his pant pockets. "I want you to pack your things — everything. I want you out of my house by morning. I don't want to hear from you. I don't want to see you. Tomorrow I will meet with my attorneys to have your name removed from my will. You want your own life — you got it. Let's see how far you get on your own without everything that I've provided for and this family. Now get out of my sight."

For a moment, Craig had stared at his father in disbelief. Dozens of scenarios and monologues raced through his head, but nothing was remotely up to the level of hurt and disappointment and, yes, uncertainty that twisted inside him. He swallowed. "Fine. If that's what you want." He'd turned to walk away so that his father would not see the burn of tears that hung in his eyes.

"No, it's what you want!" his father tossed at Craig's back. "Live with it."

That had been a little more than ten years ago. And true to his father's demand, Craig had not been back. Unfortunately, his self-imposed exile also affected his relationship with his siblings.

Alyse wrapped one hand around her glass; the other she lay flat on the table and stared at her fingers.

"Look." He reached across the table and covered her hand. "Don't get yourself all mixed up in this beef with me and Dad. It's our ugly mess, not yours."

"But we're family, Craig," she said, her voice cracking with emotion. "You're a part of that family that has been missing for over a decade."

"That's not on me." He shook his head

and glanced away.

The waitress returned with their drinks, and before they were on the table, Craig swiped up his and took a deep swallow. He lowered his head then looked across at her. "Let's enjoy the evening. We haven't seen each other in ages. Catch me up on what's going on with you and Myles."

Alyse visibly relaxed and launched into an animated monologue about her latest significant other, hirings and firings at the office and Myles's rise up the corporate ladder. "He's set to head up the new office in Detroit. As wild and crazy as the Motor City is now, real estate is a steal. There is so much potential. In another ten years that city will be unrecognizable and ready to compete with New York and LA."

"I'm sure you're right. It's definitely primed for a turnaround." He was certain that his father had seen that coming from miles away and was ready to pounce the instant that opportunity presented itself.

Their dinner arrived, and while they ate they reminisced about the crazy times they had growing up, with the conversation constantly peppered with *remember when?*

"Wow, it's nearly ten," Alyse said in amazement following her final bite of cheesecake.

"I'll drive you home."

"Don't be silly. I have my car." She grinned. "I'm a big girl now, remember."

"Yeah," he said, his voice warming. "I remember."

The valet brought her midnight-blue Lexus RX around to the front. Craig stood by the driver's door while Alyse slid in.

She glanced up at him. "When will I see you again?"

He braced his hand on the roof. "We'll work something out. Let me know when Myles is back in town and the three of us will hang out." He smiled.

"You plan on seeing Dad?" she asked hopefully.

"No."

"He misses you, you know. He'll never admit it, but I know he does."

He leaned down and kissed her forehead. "Drive safe. Love you." He stepped back and shut the door.

"Love you, too," she said through the open window then drove off.

Craig stood there until her car was out of sight. His father missed him. Hmm. He doubted that very much. It was wishful thinking on Alyse's part and nothing more. Just wishful thinking.

"Fontaine residence," Minerva said into the phone.

"Hello, this is Craig Lawson. I was hoping to speak with Ms. Fontaine."

"One moment."

Minerva put the phone down and went in search of Jewel. She was just coming down from sitting with her father.

"Ms. Jewel, there's a call for you. Mr. Lawson," she added with a twinkle in her eyes.

Jewel's heart beat a little faster, but she kept her expression neutral. "Thanks, Minerva." She came down the last few steps and walked toward the den. "I'll take it in here."

She walked in and closed the door halfway behind her, took a breath and picked up the phone. "I have it, Minerva," she said and waited to ensure that Minerva hung up the extension. "Hello," she said once she heard the telltale click. "How are you?"

"Good. Better now," he said and wished that he hadn't. "I mean, it was a busy morning. I, uh, have the revised contract as well as the shooting schedule, and the check. I wanted to drop it all off later this evening if that's okay."

Jewel grew hot all over. The tips of her ears were on fire. Flashes of their parting kiss on his last visit danced in front of her. *This evening.* Evenings were always difficult for her.

"Umm, sure. How is seven, seven thirty?" She swallowed. Her father was usually settled and calm by then.

"Not a problem. See you then."

"Okay."

"Take my cell number in case . . . of anything."

"Hang on a sec." She got a piece of paper and a pen from the table and took down the number.

"Feel free to call anytime. See you this evening. Enjoy the rest of your day."

"You, too." She squeezed the phone in her palm for a moment then returned it to the cradle and stared at the number in hand. *Call anytime.* She pushed out a breath and walked out.

"Too busy for an old friend?"

Craig slid his phone into his pants pocket and turned. "Milan." His eyes roved over her. As always, she was photograph perfect. She had the looks and simmering sexuality of a hot young starlet with the edge of maturity rolled in. Whenever Milan walked into a space, bystanders were swept up in the swirl of her aura. The magnetism that she exuded as easily as she breathed was what made her an undeniable star on the big and small screens. This role was made for her, and as much as he didn't want to stir up the coals of their past relationship, he knew that Milan would not make that easy. It was all in her eyes and the teasing flicker at the corners of her mouth. He sat on the edge of the table and folded his arms. "What can I do for you?"

Milan took a step toward him. "I think you have the answer to that."

Craig lowered his head for a moment and shook it slowly from side to side. He looked at her. The corner of his mouth curved into a grin. "Not happenin', baby. We both know that. A friendly drink is as far as it's ever going to go."

She stretched out her manicured finger and ran it along the line of his jaw. "Why? You're not seeing anyone. And we have a history. We're both going to need to unwind at the end of those *long* workdays." Her lashes lowered over her trademark smoldering eyes.

Craig stood. He looked down into her upturned face. "I'm sure you'll find something to satisfy you, but it won't be me. Not again."

Their tumultuous past flared between them.

"How many ways do I have to say I'm sorry," she begged.

"You don't. Just do what you're being paid to do." He started to move past her. She grabbed his arm.

"Craig . . . I'm sorry. When are you going to forgive me?" She blinked rapidly. "I miss you."

His cold look stripped away the facade. "You *are* good," he said, his tone dripping in sarcasm. "If I didn't know the real you and what you're capable of, I would almost believe the BS you're slinging."

Milan's five-foot-six frame jerked as if she'd been pushed. Her beguiling expression morphed into one of stunned disbelief then anger. "You don't talk to me like that," she said between her teeth.

"Milan . . . I'm not going down this road with you. Let's keep it professional. You're here for the movie, and that's it. If you've changed your mind about the role, let me know now and we'll start looking for a replacement." His unflinching gaze held her in place.

She pressed her mouth tightly together,

hurled a death stare at him and then spun away.

Craig filled his cheeks with air and pushed out a long breath. Anthony had warned him about signing Milan on to the project. But he wanted the best for the film. And, unfortunately, Milan was the best for the role. They both knew that. But, hell, he'd kick her to the curb in a heartbeat and move on if she couldn't keep the past in the past where it belonged. He never should have agreed to anything even as innocuous as drinks. Leading her on was the last thing he wanted.

"Trouble in paradise?" Anthony asked, sidling up next to Craig.

"Not anymore."

"Good. The last thing we need is diva drama. So . . . how did it go with Alyse?"

Craig smiled. "Good. Really good. We had dinner, talked, laughed — like old times."

"Glad to hear it. I'd love to see Alyse. It's been a while."

"We plan to get together when Myles is back in town. I'll let you know." They didn't talk about it, but he knew that Anthony carried a torch for Alyse. They both also knew that Alyse, unlike Craig, wouldn't cross her father.

"Sounds good. Listen, Norm wants to

meet with us for a few."

Craig nodded in agreement, but his mind was on seeing Jewel later. It was going to be a long day.

"Everything okay?" Minerva asked when Jewel exited the den.

"Yes. Fine." She tried to breeze by Minerva, but she wasn't having any of it.

"Then why do you look like a frightened doe? Did something happen?"

Jewel rubbed her hands together. "Nothing happened. He's going to drop by later to bring the revised contract and the check, that's all."

Minerva studied her. "You aren't reconsidering, are you?"

"No."

"Then what is it?"

She understood that Minerva was concerned for her. In the short time that she'd been part of the family, Minerva had taken on not only the role of caregiver but surrogate mother. A role that Jewel embraced. She'd been without a strong female figure and nurturer in her life since she was six when she'd lost her mother to cancer. Of course her father stepped in and filled as many of the empty spaces as he could, but he could never be the mother that a part of

Jewel would always miss. Although tragic circumstances had brought Minerva to them, it was also a blessing. She'd come to lean on Minerva when things became difficult and accepted Minerva's unsolicited wisdom as part of the package.

Jewel walked into the living room and sat down on the side chair. She crossed her legs at the knee and linked her fingers together. "I know financially it's the right thing to do," she began.

"But?" Minerva sat opposite her on the love seat.

"But . . . he kissed me . . . well, we kissed each other."

Minerva's eyes widened. "Really, now. Well, that changes things — or does it?" She leveled her gaze on Jewel.

Jewel glanced away. "I don't know if it does or doesn't. It complicates things, that's for sure."

"Why?"

"You know why. We've talked about this."

"No, *you* talked yourself out of it before there was a this."

Jewel pursed her lips. "Maybe," she mumbled. "But now what? What if it didn't mean anything? He's notorious for being a womanizer. I'm probably one of many. I'm sure he felt he owed it to me for saying yes to the deal," she rambled on, stacking up a litany of excuses.

"Hmm, all that, huh?"

Jewel's gaze jumped to Minerva's reproving expression. "Sounds like you are setting yourself up to be disappointed."

"But it's all true!"

Minerva shrugged. "Says the gossip sites. But you don't know that for yourself. Besides, what's so wrong with grabbing a little sunshine, no matter how fleeting? You deserve it, sweetheart. You're young, beautiful and single, but you've buried yourself in this house and under the weight of your father's illness. Do you really think Augustus would want that for you? Your father would want you to live your life and be happy."

Jewel lowered her head. "Easier said than done."

Minerva pushed up from the chair. "It's only as hard as you make it." She started to walk away, stopped and turned back. "Oh —" She pressed her hand to her forehead. "Our church committee is putting together donations for the middle school. It's a damn shame that the teachers have to go in their own pockets for supplies and such. Anyway, I was wondering if you wanted to part with any of your things in the cottage? Things you don't plan to use no more."

Jewel's stomach instantly knotted at the mention of the cottage. She swallowed. "Um, I'll take a look and let you know." She forced a smile. She knew what Minerva was trying to do.

"Whatever you could spare I know would be appreciated."

Jewel watched Minerva walk away and realized that her heart was racing. She couldn't remember the last time she'd set foot in the cottage that she'd converted into her home studio. After New York her life spiraled downward. Her relationship with Simon imploded along with her career, and she couldn't bring herself to cross the threshold of a place that represented all that she'd lost — especially her confidence. She'd lost confidence in herself as an artist and as a woman that a man wanted to commit to.

Minerva was right in some respects. She'd turned off the lights of her life, and for the first time in longer than she cared to remember, the switch turned on when she met Craig Lawson. Maybe it was time. She got up and walked out.

The cottage was situated behind the main house. Several generations ago it served as home for the servants who lived on and worked the land. She'd modernized it, adding plumbing, insulation and electricity. After a few coats of paint and some personal touches she'd made it her own. When she was in the throes and frenzy of a new project, she would sequester herself in her studio for hours and days at a time until she collapsed from exhaustion. Her father would come to look for her only to find her curled up on the floor with a drop cloth as a quilt. Eventually, she added a cushy couch and stacked sheets and blankets on a shelf for those nights when she couldn't make it the few hundred feet to her bedroom.

Those days were behind her. She knew there was nothing beyond these doors for her, even as she stood motionless in front of the cottage entrance. She swallowed down her reticence then reached into the pocket of her shift and took out the key. Her hand shook ever so slightly as she aimed the key at the lock.

Slowly she turned the key and pushed the door open. She expected to be hit with a blast of dust, cobwebs and stale air. Instead there was a lingering scent of jasmine. She stepped fully into the space and shook her head sharply in disbelief. Everything was just as she remembered it. She walked, trancelike, to her wood and metal worktable and gingerly ran her fingers across her sketchpads and the glass jars where she kept her pencils and brushes. Turning, her gaze scanned the walls that held her paintings — some completed, others mere shadows of ideas — then to the easels and the shelf that held her cameras, the cabinet where she kept her molding clays, tools and wood for her sculptures.

She pressed her nose against the stacked sheets and inhaled their recently washed freshness. That was when she noticed the vase of fresh flowers on the small table by the couch where she often slept.

Her eyes welled, and the tears slid down her cheeks. She sniffed and swiped at her eyes. She planted her hands on the curve of her hips and took another slow turn around her space. "Damn you, Minerva!" she whispered in grudging gratitude.

Jewel was frosting a wedding shower cake when Minerva sauntered into the kitchen. She'd been able to avoid Minerva for the better part of the day, but she knew it couldn't last forever.

"Dad okay?" she asked without looking up.

"He's napping. I want to get started on his dinner." She walked to the refrigerator, sidestepping the elephant in the room.

"How long?"

Minerva glanced over her shoulder. "How long for what?"

"How long have you been taking care of the cottage?"

She removed a package of chicken breasts and shut the refrigerator door. She shrugged. " 'Bout six months, I suppose."

Jewel blinked away her disbelief. "Six months?"

"Hmm. About that." She ripped open the package and turned on the water in the sink.

Jewel plopped down in a chair. "Why?"

Minerva turned and faced Jewel. "Because I believe in you even though you've stopped believing in yourself."

Jewel lowered her head. "I guess I have in a way." She pushed out a breath. "I feel like I lost my passion."

"It's still there. Buried under all the other mess that you've let pile up on you."

"Maybe."

"You'll never know unless you give it a try."

Jewel shook her head. "I . . . don't think I can go back down that road."

"You been tellin' yourself that nonsense for so long you actually believe it." She made a noise with her teeth. "Well, if you ain't gonna use that stuff in there, I'll just pack it up and take it on over to the church to distribute to the school." She opened the overhead cabinets for the seasonings and began humming something Jewel was sure was a spiritual under her breath. She seasoned, and she hummed. She prepared the chicken in the pan, and she hummed. She cut up fresh string beans, and she hummed.

"Fine!" Jewel conceded after ten long minutes of humming, the ghosts of her ancestors having challenged her with every note and a reminder that she had no idea about real hardship.

Minerva looked over her shoulder with a wide-eyed expression of innocence. "I'm sorry. What?"

"I said . . . fine. I'll keep my things." She took the frosted cake and put it in the secondary refrigerator that she used for her baking clients.

"Well, now, that's a start." She turned back to the stove.

Jewel planted her hand on her hip, slowly shook her head then walked out of the kitchen.

CHAPTER 5

Jewel stepped out of the shower and rubbed the fogged mirror clear with the edge of the towel. She stared at her reflection. Physically, she hadn't changed much in the past five years.

At thirty-two, her skin was still smooth and even, though not as bright as it once was. A stray strand of gray would pop up in her hair every now and then, which she quickly made disappear. Her eyes, wide and deep brown, haloed with long dark lashes, were reflective of her mother, her father would always say, and her thick, wild curls had been a nightmare to contain when she was growing up. Now she simply let the mass of mayhem do what it wanted. She did manage to exercise on a regular basis and she ate well, so her body maintained its original design, with a bit of extra padding around her hips and the swell of her breasts, which she attributed to age and maturity.

Fortunately gravity hadn't gotten its grip on her as of yet.

It wasn't the outside that had changed. Anyone that hadn't seen her in years would surely recognize her. It was beneath the exterior that was different. There was a huge empty space inside her that she tried to fill with the running of the house, taking care of her father and baking for a growing clientele. But when she lay alone in bed every night, the longing in that empty space mushroomed. Even when she'd been lonely or hurt or confused in the past she'd had her art to fall back on. But for the past five years she hadn't even had that to console her.

What would be so wrong in snatching a bit of happiness? Craig's kiss reminded her that she was still a desirable woman, a woman with needs. She turned away from her reflection to get ready for her evening.

It was a little after five when Jewel went to check in on her father. Minerva was removing the dinner dishes when she walked into his bedroom.

Every time she saw her father her heart twisted. She fully understood the meaning behind the phrase *a shell of a man*. Augustus Fontaine was once a robust six-foot one, two-hundred-plus-pound man, muscled from his years of hard physical labor with a spark in his eyes and hearty laugh that was infectious.

Unlike Jewel, anyone who had not seen her father in many years would never recognize him, except perhaps in those moments that were becoming more rare, when the spark of recognition lit up in his eyes and he smiled. Those moments were what she longed for each day.

"Hey, Daddy," she greeted him and pushed a smile across her lips as she walked over to where he sat by the window.

"He's having a good day," Minerva whispered as they passed each other. She patted Jewel's shoulder and walked out.

Jewel sat on the windowsill next to her father's recliner. He was staring at the apple tree outside his window. "Need to pick some of those apples before the frost sets in. Have Estelle make some pies," he said more to himself than to Jewel. "I love her apple pies."

Jewel swallowed and blinked back tears. Her mother, Estelle, had been gone so long that the only memory Jewel had of her was from pictures and the stories her father told her. She reached for her father's thin hand and brought it to her cheek. He looked up at her with muddy brown eyes.

"It's me, Daddy," she said softly. "It's Jewel."

He stared at her for what seemed like forever. He smiled. "Jewel is sho' a pretty name." His forehead tightened and his face tensed as if he was straining to grasp something just out of reach.

She caressed his hand.

"Hey, baby girl," he said clear as day. "You have dinner yet? I just finished. Pretty good today."

Jewel's heart pounded. "Hey, Daddy. No, I haven't eaten yet. I will. Wanted to check on you first."

"Don't wait till late." He shook his head. "I read somewhere that it's not good to eat late." He looked at her and frowned. A cloud dulled his eyes. "Need to get the horses in. Storm's coming." He pulled his hand out of her grip. He turned his head and stared out the window.

Jewel squeezed her eyes shut then leaned down and kissed him tenderly on the forehead. He looked at her with a mixture of confusion and gratitude. "I'll come back and check on you later, Daddy."

"Storm's coming."

She offered a faint smile. "You may be right," she murmured and walked out.

■ ■ ■ ■

"I'm not too early, am I?" Craig asked when he stepped across the threshold.

"Not at all. I'm getting set up in the kitchen. Have you eaten?" Jewel shut the door behind him.

"Uh, not really."

She threw him a smile over her shoulder. "Follow me." She led the way into the kitchen. "I'm trying out a new recipe."

"If it's anything like your muffins, I'm sure it'll be spectacular."

Jewel laughed. "We shall see. You'll be my taste tester."

His brows rose in mock alarm. "What are you fixing, exactly?" He placed the envelope with the documents on the table.

"Grilled, stuffed red snapper with a mushroom risotto and fresh green beans." She eyed the ingredients on the island table.

"I'd offer to help, but I'm not very handy in the kitchen. More of a grill man."

"Perfect. When I'm done you can slide the snapper in the grill."

"Touché."

"You can pour some wine or something stronger, if you like. The stronger stuff is in the glass cabinet in the living room. Help yourself."

"What can I fix for you?"

"There's a bottle of white wine in the fridge."

"Got it." He went off to grab the bottle of bourbon then fixed Jewel a glass of wine.

She sipped while preparing the snapper, all the while commanding her fingers to stop shaking and her pulse to slow down. If she didn't get too close to him or allow him to look right into her eyes, she would be fine. Even as she chatted mindlessly — about what, she had no idea — she simultaneously questioned why, in heaven's name, she had invited him to dinner.

"I wanted Norm, my technical director, to come by tomorrow to take some of the exterior shots of the house, the grounds and the rooms on the lower floors," Craig was saying.

Jewel took a swallow of wine. "Tomorrow. Sure." She used baking thread to sew the snapper closed. "So it begins," she said before setting down her glass of wine. She went to the sink and washed her hands. "The grill is the bottom shelf. Already preheated," she said while keeping her back to Craig.

Craig lifted the tray with the snapper and put it in the oven grill with a flourish.

"How's that for grilling?" he teased. "Told you I had talent."

Jewel turned, and he was right behind her. Her breath caught in her throat. She could see the reflection of light in his eyes and the way his dark lashes framed the intensity of his gaze.

"Need me to do anything else?"

His question sounded innocent enough, but what lurked around the corners of his mouth said something completely different. God, he smelled good. Her heart thumped. She swallowed, tried to look away but couldn't.

"I haven't stopped thinking about the other day," he said. The deep timbre of his voice strummed her insides like a plucked guitar string.

"Oh," she managed. There was no room to escape without their bodies brushing and colliding with each other. That was a no-no.

He reached out and ran his hand slowly down her arm. "It's all I've been thinking about. That's new for me," he confessed. With his other hand, he caressed the curve of her jaw. Her lids fluttered. Her heart raced.

"What about you? Has our kiss crossed your mind at all?"

She should lie. She should pretend that it

was nothing. "It has," she admitted.

"Hmm. We should do something about that." His gaze moved slowly over her face.

Jewel felt her body heat, and it had nothing to do with the oven.

And then his mouth was on hers and his arm drew her close; with his other he threaded his fingers through the explosion of her curls and pulled her to him. The tip of his tongue teased her lips, and she felt a shot of current race through her limbs.

She gave in. Gave in to the sensations, the feel of him, the taste of him. Her mouth parted to welcome him, and she felt more than heard the moan that rumbled deep in his throat.

Craig eased back, and Jewel felt bereft, as if she'd been suddenly left alone in the dark and she didn't want to be there. She wanted to step back into the warmth of light that radiated around him. She draped her fingers around his neck and leaned in, confident in her role of aggressor. But not for long.

Craig pressed her back against the sink, the hard lines of his body commanding hers to relent and merge with his. His lips worked hers; his tongue teased and danced in her mouth.

Jewel allowed herself to float on a magical ride of sensual pleasure. Every nerve ending stirred. She felt as if she'd finally been awakened after a long sleep. So what if whatever happened between them was only temporary? She deserved to feel like a woman, a desirable woman whose long-unattended needs would be satisfied.

"Jewel," he murmured against her lips before resting his forehead on hers. He released his hold on her and placed his hands on the curve of her hips. He looked into her eyes. The edges of his mouth flickered with the beginnings of a smile. "We'll never get through dinner at this pace."

His gaze was low and lazy, as if he'd been stirred from a cozy dream, Jewel thought. She pressed the tip of her finger against his bottom lip. "You're probably right." She stepped out of the space he'd cocooned them in and went to sit at the island counter. She reached for her glass of wine. Her hand trembled ever so slightly. She drew in a breath then took a long, much needed swallow.

Craig reached for the wine bottle and refilled her glass. He straddled the chair and rested his forearms across the back.

"Ply me with wine? Is that the plan?" Her fingers wrapped around the stem of the glass.

"I wish I could say I had a plan." He zeroed in on her. "I don't. I hope you understand that."

Jewel lowered her head for a moment then looked at him. "What if *I* did?"

His brow rose in question. "Have a plan?"

She ran her tongue across her bottom lip. "I wouldn't exactly call it a plan, but more like a proposal."

"Now I'm really curious."

She shook a stray curl away from her face and drew in a breath of resolve. "I'm . . . attracted to you." She swallowed. "And I believe you're attracted to me."

"Very much."

Emboldened by his reply, she continued. "You'll only be here for a couple of months at best. I'm not looking for commitment, or long term, or empty promises. I'm not in a position to ask for what I can't give in return. Once you're done here, you'll go back to your life. I get that. Totally. But . . . in the time you're here . . . let's get to know each other, explore whatever this is . . . until it's time for you to leave."

There, she'd said it, taken a leap of faith. She had absolutely nothing to lose — besides her pride, of course.

"Wow." He shifted in his seat and then studied her for a moment. "Two, three months . . ."

She nodded.

"And you're good with that?"

She nodded again. Her pulse raced.

"My time is not my own, especially when I'm in the middle of a project like this. But . . . I'll make it my business to make as much time for this as I can."

"Fair enough."

He gave her a lopsided grin and reached out and stroked her chin with the tip of his finger. "Best negotiation I've ever been involved in."

Jewel released a laugh of relief. She pushed up from her seat and stood over him. She knew what she was doing was just this side of crazy. But for once she wasn't going to plan something to death — she was going to go with the flow. So far she liked how things were flowing.

"You want to show me the contract?"

He grinned. "I want to show you a lot of things, but we can start with the contract."

Jewel served up their plates and suggested that they eat on the back veranda. Craig carried the plates, and Jewel brought the glasses and the bottle of wine.

"Oh, I forgot the salad," Jewel said. "Be right back." She darted off into the house, which gave Craig a few moments to process what had transpired.

No doubt he was totally attracted to this woman. More than he'd initially realized. But he'd never expected that she was the kind of woman who would be willing to get involved in a relationship that was transient at best. He wasn't sure what he'd expected when he kissed her, or when he made the unnecessary trip to her home. It certainly wasn't her very unorthodox proposal. He didn't know how he felt about that. A part of him, the rogue playboy part, was thrilled. But that other part that secretly longed for something that went beneath the surface wasn't as certain.

Jewel returned with a large salad bowl and placed it on the center of the circular wrought-iron table.

"Everything okay?" she asked and sat down.

"Yeah." He pushed a smile across his face. "Some work stuff I was thinking about." He relaxed in his chair. "I know you can't wait to experience how well I grilled the snapper," he teased.

Jewel giggled. "It's all in the wrist, I'm sure."

"Exactly, exactly." He cut into his fish and put a forkful in his mouth. Slowly he chewed to savor the incredible combination of flavors. "Man . . . this right here —" he pointed to the fish with his fork "— needs to be on one of those cooking shows or in some book. Wow."

Jewel grinned. "Glad you like it. After all, you did have a hand in the preparation."

He cut into another piece. "You bake, you throw down in the kitchen . . . what other talents do I need to know about?"

Her buoyant expression deflated by degrees. She focused on the food on her plate. "That's pretty much it."

"I doubt that," he said softly. "You're an artist in every sense of the word."

Jewel sipped her wine.

"That showing in New York was, what, five, seven years ago?"

Her eyes jumped to his face. She swallowed and reached for her glass. "Why?"

Craig angled his head. "You haven't been on the scene since." He'd looked her up, read about her rise in the art world and her monumental fall, the scathing reviews and the follow-up stories about how she was finished and how, almost like a self-fulfilling prophesy, she'd disappeared.

"Your point?"

"Why?"

"It doesn't matter why. That was then. I've

moved on. Let's leave it at that."

"The reviews were pretty vicious," he continued, undeterred by her stonewalling. "Was that it?"

Her expression hardened. She set down her fork and looked him in the eyes. "Let's just say it was the perfect storm of events. I made a decision, and I've lived with it. End of story."

"I work with actors every day, some of the best. I can spot a poorly acted scene a mile away. *That* was a poorly acted scene."

"What difference does it make?" Her voice rose. "Why do you care one way or the other?" Her eyes were wide.

He placed his palms down on the table and looked directly at her. "Because if I'm going to get myself involved with a woman that I am crazy attracted to . . . I want to know who she is." That was only partially true. For the most part, a woman's backstory didn't mean much for him. He rarely cared, but in this case he did. He wanted to know the real Jewel Fontaine.

Jewel bit down on her bottom lip. She turned her head and stared off into the tranquil night. A sparrow landed on the top branch of the tree, and the first splash of stars sprinkled across the sky.

"The reviews were only a part of it," she

said quietly. "My artistic sensibilities were another," she said, attempting to sound cavalier.

"As artists we're always going to be scrutinized and criticized for what we do. It's part of the game. Some critics live for the opportunity to tear an artist apart to satisfy their own lack of ability."

"I know that in a cerebral sense, but here —" she tapped her chest "— here's a different story."

Craig drew in a breath. He knew all too well what it felt like to be torn apart by the press, to have your work trampled on and dismissed. It was deeply personal, like having someone you love hurt. It was difficult enough when it was strangers, people who didn't give a damn about you as a person. But when it came from those who professed to care about you, that was a whole different kind of hurt. So yeah, he understood, but he also knew that you had to dust yourself off and keep moving.

"I know me and you are totally different. Everybody deals with their stuff in their own way. All I'm saying is a true artist, a creator never lets that go, because when they do a part of them dies inside. And on that note, I'll leave it alone." He held up his hand. "Promise."

"Thank you," she said softly.

Craig refilled her glass and then his own.

"So, tell me how you wound up selecting my home all the way from London."

He chuckled. "It was actually a pretty long process. We'd been looking for a location for about six months . . ." While they finished off their meal, he went on to tell her about the myriad of homes and locations his team had gone through in several parts of the country until Paul Frazier finally found hers. "The minute I saw it, I knew this was the place."

"What were you going to do if I'd stuck to my guns and said no?"

The corner of his mouth lifted. "In this business you always have a fallback plan. We had another potential location, but I was determined to convince you to change your mind."

"You're very persuasive."

"One of my many talents."

"Is the list of talents long?"

"And varied."

They laughed at the double entendre.

"I want to show you something," Jewel said, pushing back from the table. She grabbed the bottle of wine and her glass.

"Sure." He followed her off the veranda to the cottage behind the house.

"Hold these a sec." She handed him the bottle and her glass then unlocked the door. She flipped on the light switch.

Craig walked in behind Jewel then stepped past her and into the studio. He reverently touched the completed works and works in progress, the sculptures and the tools of her trade. He turned toward her.

"These are some of the pieces from New York."

"Hmm." She folded her arms. "A testament of sorts."

He continued to examine the works. "You were ahead of your time. It happens with all great artists." He leaned against the wall. "And the others?"

"Some ideas I had that never materialized."

"So you have been keeping up with your art?"

She heaved a sigh. "Actually, I haven't. I stuck these in here ages ago and haven't been back here . . . until today. Minerva . . . the housekeeper, unbeknownst to me, was maintaining the space."

"You had no idea what she was doing?"

"Not a clue." She sputtered a laugh. "She told me today that she was going to donate some of my art supplies to the local school and that I should come here and see what I wanted to keep. This is what I found," she added with a sweep of her hand.

"What did you decide?"

She crossed the room and sat on the cushy love seat. "I decided to keep everything."

"Will you paint again?"

"It's been so long."

"You never lose it, you know. It's like riding a bike. You just have to get back on and start peddling."

"Humph, easier said."

"Why did you bring me here, Jewel?"

She linked her fingers together and looked across at him. "I'm not sure, really."

"I think you know." He came to sit beside her.

"I spent so much time here," she said thoughtfully. "Hours, days on end when I was in the middle of creating a new piece." She smiled. "My dad finally had a bed and couch put in so that he wouldn't find me sleeping on the floor in the morning." She looked around. "This space represents my past."

"It can be your future if you let it." He pursed his lips in contemplation, leaned forward and rested his arms on his thighs. "Look, I'm not in any position to tell you what to do. What I can tell you is that when you're given a gift — and you've been given a gift — it's damn near a sin to misuse it or to keep it for yourself."

"Is that what you told yourself when you walked away from your family?"

He flinched, looked away then back at her. "Yes. It was," he finally said, the day of that decision racing through his mind. "I had a choice to make — my happiness or live in the shadow of someone else's happiness for me."

Jewel looked away. "Are you satisfied with your life based on what you had to give up?"

Craig exhaled and leaned against the back of the couch. "I won't BS you and say that there haven't been moments when I questioned myself. And it's not always easy for me to accept what I left behind in order to move forward. But I do know that if I hadn't done it, I would always second-guess myself. I would be miserable and I would blame . . . him for my misery."

Jewel angled her body on the couch so that she could face him and then tucked one leg beneath her. She sipped her wine. "Not handing all this over to Minerva's church and the local school, I suppose, is some kind of decision, in a way."

Craig looked at her and chuckled. "Yeah, kinda, sorta. It's a start." He touched his glass to hers. His expression sobered. "To starting something new."

"Something new," she whispered.

Craig put his glass down on the table and turned toward her. He reached out and tucked a curl away from her eye. "You're not like anyone I've known," he said as if realizing that idea for the first time.

"I hope that's a good thing," she said. Her voice quavered ever so slightly.

"I think so." He moved closer and plucked her glass from her hand and set it next to his. "I think that maybe this *exploration* that you mentioned is worth investigating." He leaned closer and cupped her chin, bringing her close to him. "You still good with that?" he asked against her lips.

Jewel's pulse thundered in her veins. There was still time to back out. All she had to do was move away gracefully. "Very good with that," she said instead and welcomed the pillow of his lips.

His strong arms slid around her and pulled her as close as their sitting positions would allow. His fingers stroked the curve of her spine, sending shock waves along her limbs.

Jewel moaned when his thumbs brushed along the undersides of her breasts then down the curve of her waist to her hips.

The burst of flavors from their meal was heightened by the wine as their tongues touched, danced and melded together.

Craig deepened the kiss before easing away to nibble along the column of her neck and in the V of her dress. Jewel's body quivered in response, and her breathing stopped and started.

This was so unlike her. She was always deliberate and thoughtful about getting involved. But Craig Lawson had her thinking and feeling all out of her comfort zone. Her head spun, and her body simmered. All she knew for sure was that she wanted Craig to keep stoking the flames.

Craig groaned deep in his throat. He eased back and stood. He took her hands and pulled her to her feet. "Are you sure you want this?" he rasped before dropping a hot kiss at the base of her throat.

Jewel's body shuddered. A million reasons why she shouldn't zipped through her head, but the one reason why she should beat them all to the finish line: she wanted to be reminded what it felt like to make love to a virile sexy, hot man that she couldn't stop thinking about. She wanted to feel his bare skin. She wanted his hands on her body, his body in hers. She wanted to reclaim her woman power.

"Yes," she whispered.

He looked into her eyes one last time before he possessed her mouth. He gathered her and held her tightly against him.

Jewel gasped at the erotic feel of his erection pressing against her belly a moment before Craig dipped lower and melded them together, pelvis to pelvis, rocking his hips against her in prelude of what was to come. He palmed her derriere and worked her to meet his undulations.

"Baby," he groaned against her mouth. "I want you . . . now." He eased the straps of her sundress off her shoulders and slid it down her body until the soft fabric pooled at her feet. "Let me look at you." He took a step back, and his dark eyes raked over her from the top of her head to the tips of her toes. He reached out with a single finger and outlined the curve of her breasts that flowed over the lilac lace that held them.

Jewel shivered. Her eyes momentarily fluttered as waves of heat flowed through her. Her inner thighs trembled when he stroked her there.

Craig lowered his head and stroked the valley of her breasts with his tongue. Jewel moaned and gripped his arms to keep on her feet. He reached behind her and unfastened the clasp, stripped her of her bra and tossed it aside. "Hmm," he murmured and took a turgid nipple into his mouth. His mouth suckled, and his tongue laved and teased, sending shock waves through her limbs.

Jewel grabbed the back of his head and held him in place, tossing her head back in ecstasy.

Craig turned them around slowly and backed her up toward the overstuffed full-size bed, nibbling and licking her exposed flesh in the process.

Jewel tumbled back onto the bed and looked up at him. The fierce heat and unrelenting determination in his gaze terrified as much as it thrilled her. There was no turning back now.

Craig tugged his black V-neck sweater over his head and tossed it aside. His soft, faded jeans were next. Jewel swallowed and ran her tongue hungrily across her bottom lip when her gaze landed on the imprint of his erection bulging against his black-and-white-striped shorts. He crossed the short space that separated them and made his way to her lips, beginning with hot kisses on the inside of her ankles, up her legs and behind her knees. He nuzzled her sex, and she squirmed before he dipped his tongue into the indentation in her belly.

His hands, his mouth, his tongue seemed to be everywhere at once. Jewel's thoughts scattered like windblown leaves. All that she was capable of understanding was the incredible sensations that scored her body and ignited the blood in her veins.

Craig eased her panties over her hips and down her legs. His fingers gently stroked and primed her there, and her arousal dampened his fingers. He inched his way up the curves and valleys of her body until he was pillowed between the rise of her breasts. He covered one with his palm, the other he taunted with his tongue until Jewel writhed and moaned beneath him.

She didn't know when or how, but Craig had sheathed himself and positioned his weight above her. He tenderly brushed the riot of curls away from her face and caressed her cheek. He pushed her thighs apart with a sweep of his knee and rose up on his own. The heat of his eyes moved over her face. She'd never wanted anything as much as she wanted him in that moment.

Jewel looped her hands behind his head and bent her knees. Craig pushed forward, finding her wet, open and ready. She sucked in a lungful of air as the pressure of his entry began to fill her. Her heart pounded, and she bit down on her lip to keep from crying out. It didn't work. The symphony of desire sang from the center of her being as he buried himself deep within her, hovering there to allow them both to savor that first moment.

Jewel whimpered. Her body shook as he began to move, slow and deep and steady. Bright lights flashed behind her closed lids. Waves of need raced through her. She found his rhythm and met him stroke for stroke, raising and lowering her hips in time with his thrusts.

Craig was lost on a ride of pure pleasure. Part of him wanted to pound away, take it all now, fast, and satisfy the raging need that fueled his every movement. The other part of him wanted this feeling to last forever. He could stay there forever, cocooned in her wet heat that suckled and milked him every time he moved. But as much as he wanted this to be eternity, he felt the steady building in the heaviness of his sac, the pulsing and thickening of his cock.

A deep groan rumbled in his chest. His jaw clenched.

Jewel saw the bright lights. Currents of electricity shot up the backs of her legs. Her vagina began to clench and unclench. Her breath hitched in her throat. Her fingers pressed into the muscles of his back. Her ankles locked around him. A scream burst from her lips as the first wave of her climax slammed through her and then another and another until she was delirious with pleasure, lost in delight.

Craig slid his arms beneath her hips and held her in place as he rode the final wave to his release and his body slumped against hers.

Their hearts banged and pounded against each other. Their breaths ran and danced and then mingled into one unified breath, one heartbeat.

Craig nestled his head in the sweet curve of her neck. Jewel caressed his back and the tips of his ears.

She had no words for what she was feeling. Incredible, sensational, fulfilled, joyous — nothing would explain it. She closed her eyes and held Craig close. She didn't want to think beyond today, this moment. If nothing ever came of things between her and Craig, she would always have tonight.

"You okay?" he asked in a ragged breath in her ear.

"Fine. You?"

He rose up a bit and looked into her eyes. For a moment he simply stared at her. "Better than fine," he said.

Jewel smiled. She ran a finger along his

145

bottom lip.

He reached around him and pulled up the sheet to cover them before rolling off her and resting on his back. He scooped his arm under her head and eased her close. Jewel rested her head against his chest, and the crazy feeling that this was where she belonged suddenly felt more real than she dared to hope. *Crazy,* she thought before she closed her eyes and drifted into a light sleep of satisfaction. *Crazy.*

Craig listened to her steady breathing while he gently played with a strand of her hair between his fingers. He could easily get too caught up with this woman. He'd thought that if he had sex with her then whatever it was that was making him crazy would burn itself out. If anything it had only intensified his longing. And it was far from *just* sex. He'd made love to her the way he'd wanted to truly make love to a woman for longer than he cared to remember — not just with his body but with his soul. That reality left him with an unfamiliar feeling of vulnerability. This woman had opened a door inside him and stepped in. He angled his head and watched her sleep. He kissed the top of her head and closed his eyes. *Be careful what you wish for* was the last thought that floated through his head before he drifted off to sleep.

Jewel felt herself slowly rising from the depths of satiated sleep. A comforting warmth was wrapped around her. It took a moment for her to piece together the odd weight that she felt across her thighs and realize that it was Craig's muscled leg, and that the added heat she felt radiated from him. Her heart leaped. They were so close, chest to breasts. He held her tightly against him, as if in his dreams he was afraid he might lose her if he let go.

That's what she told herself, what she would like to believe, if only for the moment. She'd forgotten what it felt like to be ravished at night and wake up with the man who had delighted in her body in the morning. She'd forgotten how decadently good that sticky feeling between her legs could be, or that subtle ache on the inside of her thighs where they'd been widened and bent to accommodate the man who rode between them.

She didn't want to make more out of what had happened between her and Craig than what it was — two adults who were attracted to each other had had sex. That was it. Her lashes brushed his chest. She inhaled his scent. Her clit twitched. That's all it was. She couldn't expect more. But for now she would make believe that this was forever. She closed her eyes, drew in a long breath of him and drifted back to sleep.

Craig dressed as quietly as he could so as not to wake Jewel. He wanted to stay and say to hell with the demands of his day and just lie with Jewel. If only it was that simple. He buttoned his jeans then pulled his sweater over his head. He stood over her for a moment and watched her sleep. It took all of his willpower not to crawl into bed with her and find his way back between the warmth of her thighs. Usually by this time he would have been long gone with a kiss and a promise to call. He shook his head and stepped into his loafers. This was *temporary.* They both knew and understood that, but a place deep in his soul kept whispering *forever.* He leaned down and placed a gentle kiss on her cheek. She sighed softly and curled tighter into sleep. Craig tiptoed out and shut the door quietly behind him.

CHAPTER 6

Jewel blinked against the early dawn light that slid between the slats in the vertical blinds. Languidly she stretched and turned on her side, expecting to see Craig. The spot next to her was empty, the sheet already cooling. She pushed herself to a sitting position and pulled the sheet up to her chin, drawing her knees to her chest. Her eyes, accustomed now to the light, moved slowly around the space. The only indication that she hadn't slept alone was the faint scent of Craig that still lingered on her skin.

She blew out a breath. Why should she have expected more? Wine and great sex. There was no reason to think that he thought any more of their encounter than that. No explanation needed, although it would have been nice, the decent thing to do.

For a moment she shut her eyes, and her mind flooded with the night they'd shared, the way her body had responded to his every touch, the power she felt in what she was able to do to him. Her body still throbbed.

Jewel tossed the sheet aside and swung her feet to the floor. No point in lying there. She had a full day in front of her. She quickly got dressed and attempted to ease back into the main house without running into Minerva. That little maneuver didn't go over very well. Minerva walked into the kitchen as Jewel inched through the front door. She felt like an errant teen coming home after curfew when Minerva's censoring gaze collided with hers.

"Good morning," Minerva said with a quick once-over. "You're up early." Her slippers whispered across the floor with her footfalls. "Breakfast?"

"Um, sure." She followed Minerva into the kitchen and took a seat at the counter.

"Coffee?" Minerva asked over her shoulder.

"Yes, thanks."

Minerva put on the coffeemaker. Jewel rooted around in the fridge for the bag of cinnamon and raisin bagels and put two in the toaster. She had a feeling the inevitable conversation would need more than coffee. She plopped down on the stool at the

150

counter and waited. But she didn't have to wait long.

"I saw Mr. Lawson's car outside last night," she said casually, while keeping her back to Jewel.

"Mmm-hmm, stopped by to drop off the new contract."

"Took a while."

Jewel bit back a smile. "Really?"

"I couldn't sleep, and I noticed the lights on in the cottage. Had to be after one in the morning. When I got up to get some warm milk about four, the lights were off, but his car was still parked."

The bagels popped up and so did Jewel. She plucked them from the double toaster and put them on plates. "Butter, jelly, cream cheese?" she asked sweetly.

Minerva swung around with her hands planted on her hips. Her eyes narrowed. "Are you going to tell me or are you going to make me beg?"

Jewel sputtered a laugh. "Fine. He spent the night. Happy?"

A slow smile spread across Minerva's mouth. "Well, it's about damned time!"

"Minerva!"

"What? It's true. You're a young woman, and he's a handsome man. And I think he likes you."

Jewel sat up straighter. "Really?"

"Of course. I can tell these kinds of things."

"Well, it's only temporary. He'll go back to London or LA when all of this is done."

"Never heard of long-distance relationship?"

"Minerva. I'm not thinking that far ahead. And I've been down the long-distance-relationship road," she said, thinking of her time with Simon. "I know how difficult it can be, especially when work comes first." She lathered her bagel with cream cheese.

"Make the most of the time you have," she said sagely. "You deserve some happiness in your life. And I like the glow."

"Glow?"

"Yes," she teased, "the glow in your eyes. I haven't seen it in a very long time. It looks good on you."

Jewel lowered her head. She did feel different. Alive. Her body still strummed from her night with Craig. But the reality was, it was just sex, and the fact that he was gone when she awoke spoke volumes.

Craig stepped out of the shower and wrapped a towel around his waist. He padded into his bedroom and went straight for his cell phone. He should have left a note for Jewel. But to be honest, his emotions were scrambled. He hadn't expected to feel the way he did — *connected.* And at first he didn't know how he wanted to handle it. They'd more or less agreed that this was a commitment-free thing. As far as he knew, Jewel still felt the same way. Now, he wasn't so sure that he did. What he did know for sure was that he wanted to see her again.

He picked up his cell phone and searched for her name in his contacts and tapped the dial icon. The phone rang and rang then went to voice mail. He started to hang up. Maybe it was a sign. Maybe she saw his name and decided not to answer. Maybe he should leave a message anyway. He pushed out a breath.

"Good morning. It's Craig. Um, sorry I didn't say anything before I left. Needed to get an early start, and you were sleeping so peacefully. Didn't want to wake you." He paused. "Uh, listen, Norm will be by later this afternoon, but, uh, I was wondering if you weren't busy this evening, maybe we could have dinner." He squeezed his eyes shut. "So, when you get a minute, give me a call and let me know. Enjoy your day. And . . . I enjoyed last night," he added softly. "Take care." He disconnected the call and tossed the phone on the bed. "What are you doing?" he chastised himself before walking off to get dressed.

After her counseling session with Minerva, Jewel finished her breakfast and cleaned up the kitchen. She had some baking orders to fill. The order details were in her phone. It was then that she realized that she didn't have it. She went to look for it and found it on the table in the hall. She must have left it there when Craig arrived last night.

When she tapped in her pass code, she saw that she had a message. Her pulse quickened. She went to her messages. It was from Craig. Holding her breath she listened to his message once, then again. Her beaming smile could have lit up a dark room. He wanted to see her again — tonight, for dinner. A date.

A wave of giddy delight rushed through her veins, and she practically skipped across the room and plopped down on the couch. Her hand shook ever so slightly as she tapped Return Call on her phone. He picked up on the third ring.

"Jewel," His voice dropped an octave. "Hello."

"Hi." Her stomach fluttered with warmth. "I got your message. Thanks for being so considerate and letting me sleep."

"I watched you for a while," he admitted.

"And?"

"And I started to crawl back in bed with you."

"You could have . . ."

"I'll remember that for next time."

Next time! She allowed herself to breathe. "Um, about tonight . . ."

"Yes?"

"What time were you thinking?"

"How's seven?"

"Perfect."

"I'll see you at seven."

"Okay."

"And this time I'll be sure I have a place in mind."

They both laughed.

"See you then," she said.

"See you."

Jewel put the phone down and rested her head back against the cushions of the couch. She closed her eyes, and a smile moved across her mouth. *What are you doing, girl?* Whatever it was, it felt good, and for now, that's all that mattered.

CHAPTER 7

As promised, Norm, the technical director, along with two other members of the movie crew, arrived at Jewel's home at noon.

"Good to finally meet you, Ms. Fontaine," Norm said. "We promise not to get in your way — or at least as little as possible." He smiled. "The plan is to take a bunch of exterior shots and shots of the first floor and of course the surrounding property. A couple of hours, tops."

"Not a problem. Where do you want to start?"

"Why don't we start inside, so we can get out of your way as soon as possible."

"Sure. I'll show you around." She took them on a quick tour of the main level: living area, den, kitchen, a small bedroom that at one time had been the servants' quarters, bathroom and the back veranda.

Norm took notes as they walked, with his two assistants trailing dutifully behind them.

He turned to Jewel. "I know I said the main level, but is it possible to see the rooms upstairs to give us more options?"

Her stomach knotted. The last thing she wanted was for her father to become upset with strangers tramping around the house. His setbacks were becoming more pronounced and prolonged, and she didn't want to do anything to make it worse.

"Well, why don't you get started down here? I have to make some arrangements."

He looked at her curiously.

"My father . . . isn't well," she said in response to his look.

He held up his hands. "Hey, not a problem. I don't want to cause an issue."

"I'll see what I can do."

"Thanks." He turned to his assistants. "Okay, fellas, let's get started. I want multiple shots of everything on this floor from various angles, full shots to close-ups."

Jewel went in search of Minerva, who was just finishing up her father's bathing. She quietly explained what the crew wanted to do, and Minerva assured her that she would keep Augustus occupied in his room — which was to remain off-limits.

"Hopefully it won't take long," Jewel said.

Minerva clasped her shoulder. "It will be fine."

Jewel crossed the room and went to sit on the side of her father's bed.

"Hey, Daddy," she said softly. She took his hand in hers. "How are you today?"

He blinked and slowly focused on her. He smiled. "Jewel. My Jewel." He squeezed her fingers. "Beautiful as ever. Just finished my bath," he said in a teasing tone.

Jewel grinned. "I bet you enjoyed it."

"Where's that young girl that works with you? Haven't seen her in a while." He frowned in concentration.

Jewel angled her head. "Mai Ling?"

"Is that her name?"

"Yes, Mai Ling. She doesn't work with me anymore."

"Who?" His gaze grew cloudy. He began to fidget.

Jewel gently patted his hand. "Mai Ling doesn't work with me anymore."

He stared at her. "I'm ready for my lunch."

Jewel sighed. She leaned over and kissed his forehead. "Sure thing, Daddy." She turned to Minerva and hoped the heartbreak that she felt wasn't reflected in her expression. "I'll let you know when they are ready to come up," she said softly. Minerva nodded.

Jewel returned to the main level and advised Norm that when they were ready she would take them upstairs.

She sat quietly on the sidelines, in total fascination, while the team took innumerable pictures. When Norm said, "from every angle," that was exactly what he got. What made the process more real was that before every final shot, a digital image was printed first so that they could be sure of every angle.

It was one thing to live and walk through your space day after day, year after year and basically not pay things much attention beyond cleaning and maybe updating furniture or draperies. It was a completely different experience to see your home through the eyes of a lens, the eyes of others.

The very unique features of her home came to life for the camera — the gleam of the wood floors, the intricacies of the crown molding, the banisters and inlays in the walls, the majesty of the sliding doors, built-in cherrywood cabinets, cathedral ceilings and crystal chandeliers. Over the years Jewel and her father had worked hard at maintaining the original woodwork, nooks and crannies right down to the claw-foot tubs and wall sconces. Of course, all of the internal workings of the house had been upgraded, but on the surface the home was very much a reflection of what it looked like more than one hundred years ago.

This home was her legacy. Allowing the filming, although intrusive, had bought her the time and money that she needed to hold on to that legacy until she could find a way to ensure a steady and substantial flow of capital. Her father and her grandparents and great-grandparents deserved to have what they'd earned maintained.

The photography took a little more than three hours. Norm thanked Jewel for her time and even left her with some of the photographs on his way out.

"You have a fabulous place. A lot of history here," he said and took a final look around.

"Thank you."

"Good to meet you. But I'm sure we'll see each other again."

"I'm sure." She stood on the threshold and watched as the team piled back into their vehicle and drove off. Jewel shut the door with a satisfied feeling. She'd made the right decision, and she was starting to believe that everything would work out.

She checked the time on the antique grandfather clock that resided in the foyer. Three hours before Craig would be there to take her to dinner. A shiver of anticipation fluttered through her, and a flash of their night together shocked her senses. There was no guarantee of how many more nights like that they would share together, but if she had anything to do with it, tonight would be another one.

Craig was on his way out of the production suite en route to his room when Milan stopped him in the hallway.

"Hey, Craig."

"Milan." He stopped in front of her.

"I was on my way to find you."

"Problem?" He shifted his iPad from one hand to the other.

"No. Not at all. Actually, I was hoping that we could make some time before shooting to . . . talk."

He tapped back the groan that threatened to escape. "I could order something up to the suite. We could chat there," he said, giving Milan a graceful way out — without him saying no — and him the distance that he wanted to maintain.

"Are you afraid to be alone with me?" she asked, taking a step to close the distance between them.

His mouth quirked with a sardonic grin. "Why would I?" His lids lowered over his eyes.

"You tell me. You've done everything short of becoming invisible any time I'm in the vicinity. I want us to be able to work together — to be friends."

"I thought that's what we were doing. I'm always available to listen to what my actors have to say." He stared at her. "Should I order up something to the suite?"

Her full lips drew into a single line. "Some other time."

He gave a slight shrug. "Not a problem." He breezed by her, covered the hall in long strides and entered his room. He was pretty sure the hot spots he felt on his back were daggers Milan was throwing.

More than once he'd questioned the feasibility of casting Milan. But artistry won out over his personal hesitation. However, he had no qualms about replacing her if things turned a wrong corner. Anthony had suggested several other actresses that could step into the role. They didn't have the name and face recognition that Milan had, and he was banking on those things to create hype for the film. With Milan and Hamilton in the lead roles, the film was guaranteed to garner the attention and box office success he knew it deserved. But he wasn't above casting an up-and-coming actress and making a star if Milan made life difficult.

He emptied his pockets on the top of the dresser then decided to send Jewel a text message before getting in the shower. He pulled up her number from his contacts.

I heard that things went well today. Great shots. We can talk about next steps later tonight. Looking forward to seeing you. C.

He hit send. Within moments the phone chirped with her response.

Looking forward to seeing you, too.

Craig grinned, pulled off his clothes and headed into the shower.

CHAPTER 8

Jewel changed her outfit three times, and she was still unsatisfied. Where were they going, exactly? She should have asked him, she worried while she took off the third dress and tossed it on the bed with the other two. He would be there in a half hour and she was still running around in her underwear. Panic set in. The room suddenly grew hot. She darted across the carpeted floor and adjusted the temp on the air conditioner. She then went to stare at the garments hanging in her closet. Again.

She couldn't recall the last time she'd gone out on a dinner date. How sad was that? After several more moments of indecision, she finally settled on a simple black dress, sleeveless, in a fabric that hinted at curves rather than defined them, with a hem that came just to her knees. Silver studs in her ears and a chunky silver-and-black rope chain for her neck.

Jewel took a step back and examined her full length in the mirror, turning right and left and of course trying to get an over-the-shoulder view. Pleased she fluffed her curls, added one more swipe of her bronzy lip gloss and a fingertip dab of her favorite body oil behind her ears and inside her wrists.

She studied her reflection. What would Craig think? Funny that it should matter. For the past few years two of the last things she thought much about were her appearance and her artistic penchant for needing approval, which had contributed to her downfall. The resurfacing of those emotions left her shaky inside, vulnerable — a place that she didn't want to ever return.

She gave a shake of her head as if to toss off the swirling thoughts and then reminded herself that it was one day, one night at a time. She truly had nothing to prove, and Craig Lawson could take her or leave her. Her gaze explored her reflection, settled on her expression, then the body encased in that dress. She smiled. Who was she kidding? For the time being, she preferred if he took her.

Craig pulled into the Fontaines' winding driveway at exactly five minutes to seven.

He would have been there earlier but he didn't want to appear as eager as he felt. He put the car in Park, peeked up at the house through the driver's side window then got out while he slid one hand into his pants pocket and strode forward. He hesitated for a moment before ringing the bell and wondered for the thousandth time why he was overthinking a simple dinner.

In concert with the bell echoing in the house, the door opened. His stomach coiled, and his heart beat just a bit faster. *Damn.* His eyes ran over her from top to bottom, taking in every delicious inch.

"Hey. Hope I'm not early."

"No. Right on time. Come in for a minute." Jewel stepped aside to let him pass.

He stealthily inhaled the soft scent of her and relished that she smelled that good all over.

"So, where did you decide for dinner?" she asked and turned toward him.

"You look incredible," he said with hunger in his voice. He stepped up to her, slid an arm around her waist and dipped his head until his mouth met hers. Jewel sighed softly. "I've been waiting for that all day," he said against her lips.

"Worth it?"

"Absolutely." His gaze rose and landed on

Minerva, who was standing at the top of the stairs.

Jewel followed his line of sight. Her face heated. She stood a step back. "Everything okay?"

"Yes, fine," she said and descended the stairs. "Good evening, Mr. Lawson."

"Good evening."

"I was coming down to fix a snack," she said to Jewel. She gave her a quick once-over. "You two have a nice time." She walked away and into the kitchen.

Jewel wished the floor would open. She slowly shook her head.

Craig turned to Jewel with a twinkle in his eye. "Ready?"

"Very." She picked up her silver-toned shawl and her purse from the table in the foyer and led the way out.

"I don't think I realized that your house-keeper lived in," Craig said as they pulled out of the driveway and onto the street.

"For about two years now."

Craig took a quick look at her profile that was set and fixed on the road ahead. He got the impression that she didn't want to talk about it. But that didn't stop him from wanting to know what caused that look on her face.

"What happened two years ago?"

Jewel's expression tightened. She tugged on her bottom lip with her teeth. "I'd really rather not. It's a long story and not very pleasant."

"I'm a storyteller. I examine life for a living. There isn't much that you could tell me that would surprise or repulse me," he added with a smile.

"I needed help with my dad," she said and offered nothing further.

When silence hung between them for a beat too long he said, "I get it. You don't have to talk about it if you don't want to."

Her expression visibly relaxed. "Thank you. But what we *can* talk about is your film."

He tugged in a breath and resigned himself to the idea that Jewel wasn't going to spill her guts — at least not yet — and for that matter neither was he. But what she didn't say was almost as important as what she did say. Clearly, there were problems with her father. Serious enough that she needed help to take care of him, which might explain a lot of things.

"Right now we're doing the table reads with the actors. The technical folks are working out logistics and scheduling, costumes and permits. This is all the behind-the-scenes stuff before the next phase kicks in."

"Which is?"

"First day of shooting."

She nodded slowly. "How much of the film will take place on the property?"

"On film it will seem like mostly all of it. But the way we have it worked out in terms of shot selection and scheduling, we should be finished shooting on your property in about a week, week and a half, tops. Unfortunately, in order to do that we start early and leave late."

"I see. What about what's not shot on the property?"

"There are street scenes and some historic sites, both of which require permits, and the rest we can finish up on the lot in LA, if necessary. I'm hoping that we can do everything here. Cuts down on time and wear and tear on the actors and won't incur extra expenses for the budget."

Craig slowed the car, peered up at the sign on the corner indicating Tchoupitoulas Street then turned. "That's the place up there," he said with a lift of his chin.

"Emeril's?" she asked, clearly delighted. The lighted logo of the world-famous restaurant promised mouthwatering delights.

He glanced at her with a self-satisfied smile. "Hope you like it."

Jewel laughed. "What is there not to like? In all the years that I've lived in Louisiana, I may have been here once — and that was ages ago. All I can remember was that the food was to die for. Since then he's opened other locations, had his own television show . . ."

"I have another surprise for you."

She snapped her head in his direction. "What?"

Craig winked. "You'll see."

He parked the car in the lot behind the restaurant, and they walked around to the front. The hostess greeted them.

"Mr. Lawson, welcome to Emeril's. Your table is ready. Please follow me."

Craig placed his hand at the low dip of Jewel's back and guided her across the restaurant to their reserved table. He helped Jewel into her seat.

"Chef Lagasse will be right out." The hostess smiled and walked away.

Jewel leaned across the table. "Wait, what did she just say?"

Craig leaned forward as well. The light of mischief sparkled in his eyes. "She said Chef Lagasse will be right out," he responded and

tried to maintain a level of utter serious-
ness.

"Very funny," she tossed back. "You know
him?"

"A little," he hedged, enjoying the delight
that he saw on her face. He would do
anything to see that kind of happiness radi-
ate from her, and to know that he was a part
of it made the watching that much sweeter.

"Fine. Play coy. It doesn't become you."
She lifted her chin in a semblance of huff.

Craig chuckled. "How 'bout I tell you the
whole story over breakfast?"

Her eyes widened. Her lips parted ever so
slightly. "Very presumptuous."

"I'm a risk taker, in every aspect of my
life." His gaze held hers steadily.

"Do you consider this — you and me — a
risk?" she asked in a near whisper.

"Definitely. But it's a risk I'm willing to
take."

Rather than respond she lifted her glass of
water and took a sip, as much to have
something to do as to extinguish the fire in
her belly.

Dinner wasn't simply dinner — it was an
event, from meeting Chef Lagasse himself
with his larger-than-life personality to being
taken into the kitchen to watch the prepara-

tion of their meal to the food itself, which defied explanation.

When they left the restaurant three hours later, they were still laughing and attempting to one-up each other with the numerous delights of the evening.

"So you met him through your cousin Rafe?" Jewel said while she strapped herself in.

"Yep. Actually, Emeril's head chef is a good friend of Rafe's. He made the original introductions, and the rest, as they say, is history." He put the car in gear. "So . . . breakfast?" He snatched a look at her.

Jewel turned to him and smiled. "I like my eggs scrambled."

"I'll see what I can do about that."

CHAPTER 9

They pulled up in front of the hotel, and the valet hurried over to take the car.

"Nightcap? I'm sure the hotel bar is still open, or I can have them send something up," Craig said while he helped Jewel from the car.

Now that she was here, the reality that she would spend the night with him in his hotel room hit home. "A nightcap sounds good . . . and your room is fine."

He led her inside and across the wide reception area to the bank of elevators. He took out his card key from his inside jacket pocket.

The doors swished open and they stepped into his penthouse suite — a setup straight out of a movie, from the pale plush carpeting, conversation seating, low-slung tables and enormous television mounted on the wall to a full bar and working kitchen.

"Make yourself comfortable, and I'll order

room service," he said. He slipped out of his jacket and tossed it on a vacant chair.

Jewel set down her purse on the glass table and rested her shawl across the thickly padded couch. She crossed the wide expanse of space to the floor-to-ceiling windows that opened onto the terrace. She opened the doors and stepped out into the warm night. The lights of the city spread out before her.

Oh, how she remembered nights like this, living like this, whatever she wanted only a phone call away, traveling, seeing the world. She sighed heavily. It seemed like a lifetime ago.

Warm hands cradled her shoulders. A soft kiss dotted the back of her neck. "I almost forgot how beautiful this city can be," Craig said into her hair.

Jewel drew in a breath and slowly turned around, finding herself surrounded by him. Her gaze rose. "It's had its share of problems. Still struggling and rebuilding, but the history will always remain."

He angled his head to the side. "Sounds like my life."

"Mine, too," she admitted with an uneasy smile.

The pad of his thumb brushed across her cheek. "What parts — the struggle, the rebuilding, the history?"

"All of it. The choices that I made . . ."

"Do you regret them?"

She lowered her head. A frown knitted her brow. She looked right at him. "Sometimes. And when I do, I feel so . . . guilty." She spat out the last word.

"But once the decision is made, we have to find a way to live with the aftermath."

"How do you do it?"

"Do what?"

She shook her head. "Never mind. It's not my business." She started to move away.

The doorbell chimed. "Room service," the voice called out.

"Be right back."

Jewel wandered back into the main living space as the waiter set up the cart.

"Will there be anything else, Mr. Lawson?"

"No. Thanks." He walked over to where he'd tossed his jacket, took out his wallet and handed over a sizable tip.

"Thank you, Mr. Lawson. Thank you very much. Enjoy your evening. Ma'am." He nodded at Jewel then quietly let himself out.

Craig lifted the covers on the plates. Fresh fruit was on one platter and an assortment of exotic cheeses and dips and paper-thin crackers on the other.

"Wow, I'm hungry all over again, if that's possible," she said eyeing the fare.

He took the bottle of white wine from the bucket, poured two flutes and handed one to Jewel.

"To making choices we can live with," he said, raising his glass to hers.

Jewel lightly tapped his glass. "To choices." She took a sip. "Hmm," she hummed. "Good stuff."

Craig walked over to the couch and sat down. He extended a hand to Jewel. She came and sat close beside him.

"You asked me how I do it," he said.

"You don't have to —"

"I want to." He looked in her eyes. "I want you to know." He took a swallow of wine, paused reflectively and said, "It's never gotten easier. I thought it would. I thought I'd get to a point where I really didn't give a damn, instead of *acting* like I didn't." The corner of his mouth flickered. He looked away. "I miss my sister and brother, my cousins. I haven't been to a family gathering in years, simply because I don't want to be in the same room with my father. So I've stayed away. I've kept busy. I've done everything that I can to show him how wrong he was about me and the choices that I made by being successful in everything

176

I've undertaken." He snorted a laugh. "None of that matters. Not once even after receiving a Golden Globe, or being on the front page of the papers, even getting my first Oscar, have I heard a word of congratulations from my father. Never."

She reached out and covered her hand with his. Jewel saw the sadness in his eyes and the pain that threaded through his words. Her heart ached for him. She could never imagine her father not being a part of her life and rejoicing in her success. "Have you ever tried to reach out to him?" she asked tentatively.

He looked away, pushed up from the couch and stood. He went to retrieve the bottle of wine and refilled his glass. "I'd been gone and out of touch with him for about three years," he began slowly, reeling in the memories. "I was in Paris when I got the call that I'd been nominated for my first Golden Globe. I just knew that if I told him, he would finally see that I'd made it, ya know."

He heaved a sigh. "So, stupid me, I called. The housekeeper answered the phone, and I told her who I was. She came back to the phone a couple of minutes later only to tell me, 'Mr. Lawson is busy. Do you care to leave a message?' I told her to tell him he could go straight to hell." He snorted a nasty laugh. "That was the last time I called."

"I'm . . . so sorry."

He waved off her condolence. "Don't be. I'm used to it."

"Are you?"

"More wine?" he replied instead.

She extended her glass. "Sure."

Craig pushed the cart closer to them, loaded a cracker with two kinds of cheeses and popped it in his mouth. He refilled her glass.

Jewel reached for the seedless grapes. "You didn't answer my question. Are you used to it?"

"I'm used to the life I've chosen. I stopped asking myself if I should have done something different or stayed here and followed my father's dream for me. I know that if I'd listened to my father, I would have grown to resent him. I would've been miserable. So . . . our relationship or lack of one is the price I chose to pay for my decision."

"It's so ironic that both of us made life-altering decisions with our fathers at the center of it," Jewel said.

"But we're on opposite sides of the equation. You've never told me in so many words, but I put the pieces together. You gave up a career for your father, didn't you?"

She hesitated then nodded.

"Maybe you'll tell me the full story . . . when you're ready." He squeezed her hand. "Me on the other hand, I pursued a career in spite of my father."

She lowered her gaze. "What a pair, huh?"

"Yeah, what a pair . . . that for all of the crazy seem to fit very well together," Craig said.

Jewel's lashes lowered over her eyes. "I think you're right . . . about the fit," she said coyly.

Craig chuckled deep in his throat. "Why don't I show you the rest of the suite." It wasn't a question. He stood, pulled her to her feet, took their glasses and the rest of the wine, and walked toward his bedroom.

Jewel followed him down a short hallway into the master bedroom. Her heart beat double time with every footfall. The lights were already dimmed, but it was clear that the massive king-size bed was the center-piece of the space. Even though it was a hotel room, it didn't have that utilitarian feel to it. It was cozy in a way, and it held the sexy scent of him. She stepped out of her shoes. There was a love seat by the window with a white shirt draped across the arm. The closet bared its holdings: an array of shirts, suits, slacks and sweaters. Several pairs of dress shoes, sneakers and work boots lined the bottom.

"The bathroom is through there," he said, lifting his glass in the direction of the partially closed door.

Jewel nodded, suddenly nervous and she didn't know why. This was what she wanted, wasn't it?

"You okay?"

She rubbed her hands up and down her arms. "Yes. Fine." She forced a smile. Her eyes jumped around the room.

Craig walked over to her. He lowered his head to look directly into her eyes. "Tell me what's wrong." He held her shoulders.

"It's silly, really."

"Most of the things that bug us are silly, but that doesn't mean they don't matter. So . . . what's up?"

She tugged in a breath and took his hands in hers. "Let's not talk about or worry about the silly stuff . . . not tonight. I don't want to think about it."

"Whatever you want." He cupped her face in his palms. His eyes roamed over her features. "What is it about you?" he murmured in wonder. His eyes narrowed. "I've told you things I've never told anyone," he confessed.

"Is that a bad thing?"

"I hope not. I don't want it to be."

She studied him for a moment. "It's not only your father that did damage, is it?"

Craig took a step back. "That's definitely a conversation for another time." He turned away and walked toward the lounge chair. He slung a hand into his pocket. Jewel came up beside him and slid her arm around his waist. She rested her head on his shoulder.

"Another time, then," she whispered.

Craig turned. He threaded his fingers through her hair, loosening the curls to flow around her face and neck. He palmed the back of her head and pulled her toward him. No more words, no more hesitation. His mouth covered her lips, and he sucked in the sigh that floated up from her center and ignited his.

His arousal from her nearness kept him on simmer all night, but now that he had her in his arms, had tasted her again, felt the curves of her body melt into him, his response was swift, hard and throbbing.

He pressed against her, wanted her to feel what she had done to him, how crazy she'd made him. He reached behind her and unzipped her dress, peeled it away from her shoulders and down her frame until it fell to her feet. Her black bra was next. He tossed it onto the chair and took a half step back to look at her. Lowering his head he nuzzled the swell of her breasts. Her body shook, and a soft whimper escaped her lips.

Craig eased down her body, planting light kisses along her exposed skin until he was on his knees. He slid his fingers around the band of her panties and pulled them down to her ankles and then tasted her.

"Ooh!" Jewel gripped his shoulders. Her thighs trembled with each flick and stroke of his tongue.

Craig gripped her hips and held her fast, feasting until her trembling and soft cries were more than he could take. He rose, tugged off his shirt. Jewel unbuckled his belt and slid down his zipper. Craig stepped out of his slacks, toed out of his shoes. Jewel stepped over her dress and panties and backed up toward the bed, pulling Craig along with her.

Jewel scooted up to the top, Craig following until he hovered above her.

He pushed her hair away from her face, kissed her forehead, her cheeks, and her mouth. His hands were everywhere. Jewel writhed beneath him, wanting him, letting him know the depth of her desire with each rotation of her hips.

Craig snatched up the thick pillow and

shoved it under her hips. He rose up on his knees and reached over into the nightstand for a condom.

Jewel took it from him, tore it open with her teeth then slowly, erotically rolled the sheath down his length, much to Craig's delight.

He clasped her hips tightly in his hands. Jewel bent her knees. He lowered his head and tenderly kissed her, holding them both in a moment of unbridled anticipation. And then he was inside her.

Air rushed out of her lungs in a gasp. Her eyes slammed shut. He filled her, and in that moment, their initial coupling was more intense than the first, if that were possible.

In unison they moaned and sighed as pleasure whipped through them and they found their beat, slow and steady, hard and soft, meeting each other stroke for stroke.

Jewel clung to him, gave herself up and over to him. Her body came fully alive, vibrated from the inside out. She could barely think; her breath hitched, her heart pounded. She wanted him, all of him. She wanted him so deep inside her that he touched her heart. So when he lifted her legs and draped them across his shoulders, leaving her wide-open and vulnerable to his every move, tears of *yes, yes, yes,* sprang from her eyes. She buried her face in his neck and held on as the first wave of her climax began at the soles of her feet, shimmied up the backs of her legs, vibrated in her thighs, pooled in her pelvis and exploded with such power that the room spun. Her breathing ceased, and a scream clung in her throat until the next wave hit her with such force that her body stiffened as if electrocuted, and the sound that burst from the center of her being sent Craig up and over the edge of this world and into the next.

His head dropped onto the pillow of her breasts. He muttered a curse of disbelief as the final throes of release pumped through him.

Jewel lay curled against Craig's side with one leg draped across him while he gently caressed her, intermittently kissing her hair. So many thoughts scrambled in her head. She didn't want to get used to this, to need this. But it would be so easy. For as much as Craig Lawson wore the armor of the uncommitted, she sensed that there was a part of him that wanted more, that wanted to be connected. He claimed that he had no desire to forge a relationship with his father, yet everything that he did smacked of his need to have that void in his life filled. Even if he was only temporarily with her. She felt the longing in him every time he pushed into her, moaned her name. It was not only physical. He wanted a connection, to belong to someone.

Or . . . maybe it was all wishful thinking on her part. Projecting her own wants onto him. She closed her eyes. But even if she could make it true, what could she offer a man like Craig Lawson when she had her own empty places to fill?

They had breakfast in bed and watched the morning news like any other couple before enjoying a joint shower and one more romp for the road under the pulsing water.

Jewel sat on the side of the bed and put on her shoes.

"I really don't want you to go," Craig said and sat down next to her. He caressed her cheek.

Her eyes roamed over his face, wishing that it were true.

"I would drive you back, but duty calls and I'm already late. I have a full day today. I called a car service for you. It should be downstairs in a few." He grabbed a shirt from his closet and slid it on. "If you're not busy . . . maybe later tonight?" he asked with a note of hesitation as if bracing himself for her to say no.

"Call me." She could not allow herself to fall into the trap of being so readily available, something for him to do while he was in town, even if she wanted to leap into his arms and say yes.

He leaned down and kissed her. "Will do."

She picked up her purse and shawl and met him at the door. "Now for the walk of shame," she joked.

"Baby, you could put the walk of shame to shame any day." He swung her in for a long kiss before inserting his card key into the elevator.

They parted at the taxi with Craig promising to call later. As the car pulled off, Jewel looked behind her, hoping like in the movies that he would be standing there . . . watching, waving. But he was already gone.

CHAPTER 10

"Who was that?"

Craig stopped short and turned to his right. Milan was sitting in a club chair by the front door. He drew in a breath of annoyance. Milan pushed up from the chair and walked over to him.

"Long night?"

"Twenty questions. And why does it matter?" He continued toward the elevators with Milan keeping pace at his side.

"It doesn't. I was only asking. She's cute, in an ordinary kind of way. Doesn't seem like your type."

The elevator doors opened. Milan stepped in.

"You wouldn't know anything about my type." He stepped back as the doors began to close. "I'll catch the next one."

The minute the words were out of his mouth, he regretted them. He knew that he needed to keep his cool and not antagonize

Milan. The last thing he wanted was for her to have one of her diva fits on set because she was pissed at him. There was no telling how she would react when she realized that the woman she saw him with was the owner of the home where the filming was to take place. Any other time he would have handled things differently, taken her to dinner and maybe even to bed. But now . . . He heaved a sigh, stabbed the button for the elevator and ran a hand across the close cut of his hair. Now things were different. He was going to have to find a way to make nice with Milan. Inwardly he groaned.

Jewel had no reason to feel like an errant child when the car pulled up onto her property. She was a grown woman. Hadn't Minerva told her as much? She'd all but given her seal of approval on Craig Lawson. So why was her heart pounding in anticipation of Minerva's all-knowing look?

She walked up the three steps to the front door, turned the knob and peeked her head in before slipping inside. Humming came from the kitchen. She pulled in a breath and pranced into the kitchen as if she always walked in the door at 10:00 a.m. with her evening clothes on.

"Morning," she sang.

Minerva turned from the sink, shook out her wet hands and reached for a towel. "Well, don't you look nice for this hour," she teased.

Jewel dropped her purse on the counter and sat down. "I don't want to care about him," she blurted out, suddenly needing the wisdom of the older woman. She looked at Minerva with wide eyes.

Minerva sighed. She put the towel down by the sink. "There is nothing wrong with caring about a man other than your father. He's the only man who has been in your life for the past five years. I'm not saying that he shouldn't be, but there needs to be more in your life. Your last adult relationship was with Simon."

Jewel looked away. She knew that part of her hesitation was her fear of being hurt again, after investing so much of herself like she did with Simon. That was part of her rationale for getting involved with Craig. She knew it was temporary — there wasn't the possibility of long term and the problems that went along with it. But somewhere in her grand scheme, someone had flipped the script. She was beginning to feel again, to want something for herself again. And it scared her.

"I'm not sure what I should do, Minerva.

From the moment we met, something happened. It was like a switch got turned on. My thoughts are clouded with him. But I can't let this schoolgirl crush screw up my head."

"The heart is going to do what the heart is going to do. No matter how hard you try to fight it." She stretched out her hand and took Jewel's. "Enjoy it for what it is. If it's destined to be more than temporary, then it will be. If not, well —" she gave a short shrug "— it's what you expected anyway."

Jewel blew out a breath, then a slow smile bloomed across her mouth. "Guess where we went last night?" She went on to regale Minerva with the incredible meal and actually meeting Emeril. She took the story as far as arriving at the hotel and left the rest to Minerva's active imagination.

"I hope you used protection," she said, wagging a warning finger.

Jewel's face flamed. She popped up from the chair. "I think this conversation has gone on long enough. I'm going to change and then spend some time with Dad."

Jewel listened to Minerva chuckling as she headed up the stairs to her room.

The day seemed to drag by and the late afternoon shower made it dreary as well.

For the first time in quite a while, Jewel felt restless. She wanted to do something. Energy whirled around inside her, filled her head and tingled her fingers. She thought of baking but couldn't drum up the enthusiasm.

She grabbed an umbrella from the stand by the door and headed out to the cottage.

"What the hell did you say or do to Milan?" Anthony asked Craig when the crew broke for lunch. "She's been on a tear all morning. You should have seen her at the table read."

Craig's jaw clenched. "She saw me this morning."

"And?"

"Leaving the hotel with Jewel."

"Aw, hell, man."

Craig's face tightened. "Don't start. I'm not in the mood for a lecture." He dropped the script on the table, crossed the room to the minibar and opened the small fridge. He took out a bottle of beer. "Want one?"

"Naw, I'm good."

He opened the bottle and took a long swallow.

"Look, man, do what you want with whomever you want, but don't leave dust and debris in your wake. Jewel seems like a real lovely woman. She's not like the others. And you've been down the road with Milan. You know what she's like and how she can get, especially when she thinks that someone is taking her shine."

"There's no shine of hers to be taken. Me and her are past tense."

"Doesn't matter with someone like Milan. You know that."

Craig flopped down in the chair and turned the bottle up to his lips. He stretched his long legs out in front of him. "I really got a thing for her, man," he admitted. "First I figured it was just physical, ya know." He shook his head. "It's not. I want to be with her. I enjoy her company, the way she makes me feel. Easy. Not like I have to measure up to some ideal."

"That's cool and I can get with that, but, bruh, you ain't gonna slow down. You sure as hell ain't gonna settle down here, of all places. So how's that gonna work?"

Craig looked away, finished off his beer and stood. "I'll work it out."

"I sure hope so. We got a lot riding on this film. Not just you . . . all of us."

"Yeah, I know."

Once she got started, the embers of her passion ignited. Shape, color, context all came together in swift, sure strokes. There were times when she thought she'd lost the ability to create this way, but she hadn't, and the realization continued to fuel her. Hours passed, and when she finally sat back and looked at what she had done, her eyes filled with tears of joy.

It was him come alive on canvas. She had managed to capture the resoluteness of his jaw, the wide sweep of his brow, the curve of his lips, the penetrating, almost brooding stare, but most of all she had encapsulated what emanated from him — vulnerability cloaked in power. Beyond the probing gaze was a look of longing, something that was just out of his reach.

The portrait was in charcoal and pencil. It would serve as her base when she replicated the piece in oils.

Exhaustion suddenly overwhelmed her. Giving birth to her first creative work in years had drained her physically and emotionally. Her hands trembled ever so slightly as she returned her instruments to their cases, and her legs threatened to give out when she stood.

She dragged herself over to the couch, flopped down and stared at what she had done, realizing then that the only light came from her lamps. The day was gone, and night had taken its place. How many hours had it been? She should go back to the house. But she wasn't ready. Not yet. She needed to savor this moment of accomplishment. Sit here for a few minutes more. Her fingers still tingled with electric energy. A giddy joy bubbled in her stomach. Her lids fluttered against her will. She stretched and yawned, leaned her head back. She needed to close her eyes. Just for a minute.

Her last thought before she drifted off into a deep sleep, with his lifelike image looking down on her, was that Craig had not called as he'd promised.

CHAPTER 11

"You want anything else?"

"Maybe another glass of wine," Milan said.

Craig signaled for the waiter, who brought another bottle and filled their glasses.

"Thank you for dinner," she said sweetly. She took a sip from her glass.

"It's the least I could do. I wanted to clear the air between us."

She lowered her fake lashes and puckered her polished lips. "We have a history, Craig, one that I can't easily forget. I know I messed up. I only want you to forgive me and maybe . . . give us a second chance."

He wrapped his hands around his glass. "Listen, Milan, like I've been telling you, there's nothing to forgive. Really. What happened is in the past, and we've both moved on."

"What if I haven't?"

"That's what I need you to understand,

Milan. I didn't ask you to take this role in the hopes of us getting back together. I wanted you for this part because you're the best actor for it and I believe this will be a career changer for you."

"Is it because of her?" she challenged.

Craig pushed out a breath and asked himself yet again why he had bothered. But Anthony kept at him to make peace with Milan before things turned ugly. So he'd asked her to dinner, to talk, to make the peace. Where he really wanted to be was with Jewel. It was nearly eleven. He'd promised he'd call her, and he hadn't. If he were honest with himself, he would admit that part of the reason why he hadn't called was that he felt himself moving into the deep end of the pool with Jewel. He could have taken Milan to lunch. But instead he took her to dinner to make things right between them. Now he regretted his decision.

"Well, is it?" Milan pressed.

Craig snapped back to attention. "Is it what?"

"Is it her? Is she the reason why there can't be an us?" She placed her palms flat down on the table.

"Milan . . ." He shook his head in frustration and ran a hand across his chin. He leaned forward. "It can't work." He softened his voice. "It can't. And it has nothing to do with her."

Milan lifted her chin and turned her face away. "Fine," she whispered.

"I need things to be cool between us. We have to work together. We have a job to do, and I am depending on you to make this movie a success," he added, playing into her vanity.

"Fine," she said again then turned to face him. "It's getting late." She made moves to get up.

"Look, there's something you need to know before we get to the set."

She stopped. "What?"

"The woman that you saw me with. She's the owner of the house where we'll be filming."

It had been two days and she hadn't heard from Craig. More than once she picked up her phone to call him but decided against it. Maybe it was for the best. She'd felt herself falling, but she'd caught herself before she hit bottom.

At least that's what she told herself until the cavalcade of SUVs and equipment trucks arrived.

Jewel stepped out onto the landing of her

house. Her heart raced. Car doors opened and shut. Her pulse thundered in her ears. Her eyes skipped over the moving bodies hoping to see him among them and not wanting to see him at the same time.

It was clear that after everyone had disembarked from the vehicles that Craig was not among them.

"Good morning, Ms. Fontaine," Anthony greeted her, coming up on the landing and extending his hand.

Jewel shook his hand. "Nice to see you again. Well, I guess this is it, huh?" she said, watching the unloading process.

"I promise to make this as painless as possible. Today we're going to get the exterior shots done. Unfortunately, tomorrow we'll have to get started about 7:00 a.m., and we'll be inside shooting most of the day."

"Sure. Craig . . . Mr. Lawson gave me the schedule."

"Great. As soon as the lighting techs set up, we'll get started."

"I'll let you get to it. If you need anything, I'll be upstairs."

"Thanks. We'll be fine. The equipment trunks are like home away from home. We have everything we need." He turned away and began shouting orders to the crew who were now spread over her property like fire ants.

Disappointment mingled with relief. Jewel went back inside and shut the door behind her. Minerva met her in the foyer.

"What's wrong?"

"Nothing," Jewel murmured. "Too late to second-guess."

"Is he here?"

"Who?" she asked, although she knew exactly who Minerva meant. "No," she conceded.

Minerva squeezed her shoulder. "And when he does show up, which he will, you'll be just fine."

Jewel smiled and continued on upstairs.

His plan was to lag behind so that by the time he arrived on set everything and everyone would be in place and ready. He would have no other choice than to get right to work. Work would consume his focus and all of his energies, and he wouldn't have the time or opportunity to look for or spend time with Jewel. If he had his way, he'd spend all of his time with Jewel. But there was no room for distractions. And she was most definitely a distraction, in the best kind of way.

That was part two of his master plan. Part

one was to keep his distance and not contact her. It had been hard as all hell, but he'd managed. He had to be totally focused on the film. The quicker he did his part, the sooner he could open his mind to his "distraction." Two whole days, and it took all of his willpower to stay on task and not pick up the phone and call or get in his car and drive over. But he'd made a decision. There was too much on the line, and the person he needed to keep happy and appeased was Milan — for everyone's sake.

After their dinner the other night when he'd told her who Jewel was, Milan had one of her epic tantrums, causing a major scene in the restaurant.

"You think I'm an idiot!" she'd screamed. "I know you're screwing her. It's what you do! Is this how you punish me — by throwing her in my face day after day!"

Every eye in the restaurant had been glued on them. He could tell by the expressions on some of their faces that they recognized Milan. Cell phones came out. This latest public display would be all over the internet in minutes.

Craig had taken her by the arm and hustled her out of there, trying to keep his head down while blasting Milan out under his breath. By this time she'd dissolved into hysterical tears.

She really was crazy. That was the only thought running through his head as he'd whisked her past the curious onlookers and into the waiting car.

He pushed the nightmarish episode out of his head as he pulled onto the Fontaine property and parked his Suburban behind the line of cars. He, as well as the attorneys, had advised Milan that any further public outbursts would result in her being removed from the project as a breach of the morals clause. Apparently when she'd signed on, she didn't pay attention to the fine print. Knowing what Milan was capable of, Craig had had that little caveat included to protect him and the project.

But he couldn't take chances on pushing any of Milan's many buttons. She was crazy enough not to give a damn just to hurt him. *Artists.*

He hopped out of the car, scanning the grounds for any sight of Jewel. Part relief and part disappointment filled him. He strode toward Anthony. He had work to do, and he couldn't do it with Jewel Fontaine on his mind.

Jewel watched the magic of moviemaking from the safety of her father's bedroom window. Then Craig came into view. Her heart kicked up a beat. She gripped the edge of the window frame, willing him to look up and hoping that he didn't.

She watched him orchestrate the symphony of people and equipment and was mesmerized by the flow of authority that he exuded.

"Who's coming? I hear voices," her father said.

Jewel turned away and went to her father's easy chair that faced the back windows of the property. She knelt down beside him and took his hand.

"It's okay, Daddy, just some folks in the yard. They're making a movie." She smiled at him.

Augustus's cloudy eyes narrowed. "Whatchu mean, movie?"

"Some people thought that our house would look beautiful in a movie about an old Southern family."

He grumbled and began to pat his hand on the arm of the chair. "Gotta be careful," he hissed suddenly. "Be careful."

"About what?"

He turned to her and blinked slowly. "I think I want toast this morning."

Jewel sighed with a sad smile. She kissed his forehead. "Sure thing, Daddy, just the way you like it. Every day."

"Good morning," Minerva said from the doorway then walked in. She carried Augustus's breakfast tray.

"Morning, Minerva. Let me help you with that." She walked over and took the tray. Under her breath she said, "He seems okay about the hoopla downstairs. Just told me to be careful." She laughed lightly.

"Father knows best, even when he doesn't seem to know a thing," she said in return. She took the tray back from Jewel and went to her charge.

Jewel frowned. She started to ask what she meant but decided that she couldn't deal with two cryptic people and subliminal messages in one setting.

"I'm going down," she announced.

Minerva waved, and Jewel swore she heard her father mumble something about some pretty young girl in his room.

She trotted downstairs and went into the living room. She turned on the television to catch the morning news with the hope of blocking her thoughts from the activity on the other side of her door. She settled on her local news channel just as the entertainment portion came on air. She'd made it a point to steer clear of celebrity news and social media sites after her own debacle on the world stage. But for now it was simply mindless activity. As usual there were the stories and images of celebrities doing what celebrities did. And then Craig's face popped up on the screen in a box behind the newscaster's head.

"Two nights ago, award-winning film-maker and New Orleans' own prodigal son Craig Lawson was seen up close and personal with his leading lady, Milan Chase, as they left the Brasserie Restaurant after what appeared to be a lovers' spat." The screen flashed images of them hustling out of the restaurant and into a black car, with Craig holding on tightly to Milan's arm. "As many of you know, Lawson and Chase were a big item several years ago when she had a small role in one of his films. Neither of their reps were available for comment. But we can't help but wonder if the explosive couple will be another Brad and Angie."

The woman's voice droned on about the next hot item, but Jewel had stopped listening. She felt sick. Her temples pounded. Two nights ago, he'd promised to call. Two nights ago she'd poured her soul into recreating him on canvas, almost as an homage to what was blooming between them. Two nights ago, he was with *her*. He was no different than Simon. He hung around for as long as it suited him. What she felt didn't matter.

She pressed her fist to her mouth, but it barely held back the sob that escaped. What a fool she'd been. She'd fallen for the voice, the swagger, the looks, the touches, the sex and the aura of mystery. But she shouldn't have. They'd agreed. It was just a temporary thing. Little did she know that to *him* temporary only meant days. He and that woman had a history. They had the kind of life that she'd given up. There was no way that she could compete with that, and she wouldn't.

Jewel wiped her eyes, reached for the remote and turned the television off. *Gotta be careful. Be careful.* Maybe her father knew and understood more than she did.

CHAPTER 12

He had yet to see her, and as much as he forced himself to stay focused, he couldn't help but wonder where she was. Anthony said he'd spoken with her earlier. Maybe she'd left the property and was waiting for them all to leave before she returned. He wouldn't blame her. His behavior toward her was the kind of shitty conduct he didn't want to be known for. She deserved better. At least Milan was acting like the professional he knew she could be. Her scenes were flawless, and the camera loved her just as he knew the audiences would.

They would lose the optimum light for the daytime scenes in about an hour. Craig wanted to get the last scenes shot quickly and wrap for the day.

"Okay, people," he shouted to get everyone's attention. "We're going to shoot this last scene out of sequence. I want to get the light. Hamilton, Milan, this is your big parting scene. Neither of you are sure if you will ever see each other again. You vow to wait, no matter what. This is emotion filled. I want the audience to feel your pain, your fear and your love for each other. Okay, let's go, people!"

He waited for the crew to reset the scene and for Milan and Hamilton to get their makeup touched up before they got a last look at the script. He took a look at the scene through the viewfinders of the three cameras to ensure they got the angles that he wanted.

"Been a great morning," Anthony said, coming up alongside Craig.

"Feeling real good about this, bro." He turned to his friend and grinned.

Anthony clapped him on the back. "You should. This has awards written all over it. And . . . I hate to admit it, but you were right about Milan. She's pitch-perfect. Crazy but talented," he added with a chuckle.

"Yeah." Craig laughed as well. "You're right about that. I'm just glad we were able to nip her crazy in the bud."

"So, uh, what about Jewel? You think she's seen any of the pictures or stuff on the news about the other night?"

Craig's jaw clenched. He pushed out a

breath. "I'll work it out." He turned his attention to the production. "Okay, let's get this done."

It took almost an hour after shooting the last scene for the crew to pack up the equipment and for the principals, supporting actors and extras to pile into the waiting vehicles and drive off. By then twilight had settled, that in-between time when reality seemed to mix with fantasy.

Jewel dared to open the front door and step outside. She looked around, and it was as if all those people had never been there. It was hard to believe that mere hours earlier the grounds had been covered with lights, people, cameras and cables that ran like snakes across the grass.

She walked over to the swing bench and sat, took her cell phone from the pocket of her shorts and set it beside her. She had successfully avoided contact with Craig all day. Or maybe it was the other way around, because it was Anthony who came to advise her of the progress and when they were leaving. It was him that thanked her for her hospitality and promised to respect her home when they returned in the morning. She pushed up from her seat and returned inside. Maybe a hot shower would wash away her need for Craig Lawson.

Craig lounged in the armchair and stared out the hotel window. He sipped on a glass of bourbon and let his mind wander through the events of the day. No matter how hard he tried to stay focused on the success of a day of filming, his thoughts continued to shift to Jewel. It seemed that the harder he tried to keep her — and them — in the background, the more she continued to sit on the forefront of his mind. The whole staying away agenda was futile. Even though they weren't physically together, she was still with him — deep inside. It would be difficult, that much he was certain of. But somehow he would make it work.

He tossed back the last of his drink and set the glass down on the side table. Enough of his self-imposed mind game. He wanted Jewel in his life. End of story.

The crew was back the following morning to finish up some of the final scenes. Jewel intentionally stayed out of sight, only peeking out at the unfolding of shooting from the second-floor window. They worked until they lost daylight and finally called it a day.

When all the cars and trucks were gone, Jewel dared to step outside to reclaim her space. A wave of sadness swept through her. She shouldn't have wished that Craig would seek her out to tell her how much he missed her or that Milan meant nothing to him. She was a grown woman and had gone into whatever it was that was happening between them with open eyes. Eyes that, she admitted, had been temporarily clouded by her long-buried desire to be loved again. And she'd foolishly allowed herself to think that it could be Craig.

Deep in her musings and caught in the blur of dimming light, she wasn't sure if it was an image walking across the grass or the movement of shadows until the figure fully formed in front of her. Her breath caught in her lungs. Her stomach knotted.

Craig strode up the short incline and stopped several feet away from the porch landing. "I parked on the street," he offered with a toss of his head behind him, as if it was some kind of explanation. "I wanted to wait until everyone was gone."

"For what?" she asked.

"I wanted to talk to you."

"As I said, for what?"

Craig took a step forward and stopped in anticipation of her telling him to stay put, but she didn't. So he kept walking until he stood on the top step of the landing. He shoved his hands in his pockets. The evening light illuminated for him the emotions that flickered in her eyes — anger and hurt. He'd put that look there, and she didn't deserve it. She deserved his honesty, but he didn't know where to begin.

"Can we go for a walk?"

"No. You can say whatever it is you have to say from right there."

He lowered his head for a moment then looked right into her accusing stare. "I don't know what you've seen or heard about . . . me and Milan Chase." He saw her nostrils flare for an instant. "But nothing is going on."

"Why should that matter to me? You're a grown man. No strings, remember."

Inwardly he flinched at the chunk of ice she'd tossed at him.

"I don't need your . . . whatever this is you're doing, your mea culpa. We're both in the business of images. Remember? Pictures tell tales." She snatched up her cell phone from beside her and went through a series of clicks then turned it to face him, swiping from one picture to the next. Images of him and Milan with her hand on his, another with their heads close together, one of her laughing at something he'd said, then the infamous rush from the restaurant and into a waiting vehicle.

She smiled, but there was no joy in it. "As I said, what do you want? Oh, wait, let me rephrase that. You got what you wanted, so just go." Her voice cracked. She blinked rapidly.

Craig was next to her in a heartbeat. Roughly he pulled her to her feet, wrapped his arms around her and captured her mouth with his. He wanted to embed his feelings into her, burn into her memory that what was going on between them was real, that what he was feeling for her was real, and none of that other crap mattered.

The phone clattered to the floor.

Craig groaned when she melted into him. His arms looped around her to cup her head in his hands and seal his mouth to hers. He felt her heart bang and hammer, his thoughts swirled. There was no turning back now.

They sat shoulder to shoulder on a flat rock overlooking the brook that ran behind the house. A warm breeze blew around them. Craig linked his fingers between Jewel's and slowly and honestly told her about his past relationship with Milan, his reasons for hiring her and what really went on at the restaurant.

"I've been telling her since day one that we were done and that our relationship was strictly professional." He pushed out a breath. "But she kept it in her head that she could change all that. Her performance the other night was the last straw. I had our lawyers contact her agent to remind them that we would invoke the morals clause if she stepped out of line again during filming." He waited a beat. "I need to tell you all of it."

She whipped her head to face him. He held up his hand. "It's not whatever it is you're thinking. The real reason why she flipped the other night was because of you."

"Me? What are you talking about? I don't know the woman." Her expression twisted in confused outrage.

"She saw me put you in the car when you spent the night at the hotel. She asked me about you and if you were the reason why I refused to be with her."

"And . . . what did you tell her?"

"That it was none of her business. I also told her that you were the owner of the house. She pretty much lost it after that. Said some pretty ugly things." He lowered his head then looked at her from an angle. "I never meant to hurt you, Jewel. Never. I need you to believe that." He squeezed her fingers. "I know that we don't have a lot of time and I have no idea how things are going to work out when I'm done here, but I want you to believe me when I tell you that whatever time I have, I want to spend it with you."

"I do, too," she confessed and felt as if a boulder had been lifted off her chest. A smile beamed across her mouth. "So do I."

Craig leaned in and kissed her so tenderly that she felt as if her heart would break into a million pieces of joy.

Jewel leaned back and stared at him, let her eyes take him in. Yep, she'd done him justice, she concluded. "Come, I want to show you something." She took his hand, and they walked together to the cottage.

She switched on the lights and walked him around to the front of the canvas that took up the center of the floor.

His mouth opened then closed. His eyes registered his amazement.

"This . . ." He looked at her then back at the portrait of himself. "It's incredible," he managed. He stepped closer. "It seems alive . . . I seem alive . . ." He laughed. "I don't know what I mean." He whirled toward her and clasped her shoulders. "Baby, you have a gift." He leaned into her.

"A God-given gift, and it's gotta be some kind of mortal sin not to share it with the world. You need to do this. This is you. It's in your soul. You're an artist down to the marrow of your bones."

Jewel pressed her lips together to keep from crying. It had been so long since she even dared to feel that way about herself and longer since someone told her. The feeling was overwhelming.

"It's okay to cry," he said, wiping a tear away with the pad of his thumb. "Tears of happiness, I hope."

She nodded vigorously and sniffed.

Wrapped in his arms she shut her eyes. This could be the real deal with him if she let it happen. And if he did the same.

CHAPTER 13

Filming continued for the next week with at least another week until completion of the interiors. The schedule was grueling, as it didn't end with cut but continued into the nights, when the dailies were reviewed. But as promised, Craig spent whatever time and energy he had with Jewel. While he worked on set, she worked in her studio, pouring years of pent-up creativity onto canvas. Whether he knew it or not, Craig had given her part of her life back.

They shared dinners at her home, moonlit walks and phone conversations late into the night. It was agreed between them that they would keep their relationship private. The last thing he wanted was for Jewel to become fodder for the tabloids and speculation about his love life. Not to mention that he needed to keep Milan in control. It was a delicate juggling act.

But leave it up to his sister, Alyse, to add

her drama to the mix.

"If I had to wait for you to call me, we would never speak," she chastised.

Craig gripped the phone in his hand and inwardly groaned. "Sis, you have to know how busy I've been. We're right in the thick of things right now."

"According to TMZ you certainly are with that . . . woman. Craig, how could you? You know what she's like. I know she was your rebound after Anastasia, but she's bad news."

"It's not what you think."

"Oh, really? Then what is it? You're back in bed with her, aren't you?"

"No! Christ. Give me a little credit. I'm not involved with Milan Chase. I'm seeing someone else," he blurted out before he could stop himself. *Dammit.*

"Oh, really? Who?"

"Alyse . . ."

"Tell me, who is it?"

"Her name is Jewel Fontaine."

There was a moment of silence on the line.

"Her name sounds familiar. Wait, *the* Jewel Fontaine? The artist? Wait. Hold up. She owns that house. The one you're filming at! It was in the paper."

Craig didn't respond. He already knew he'd dug a big hole for himself. All he could hope was that he didn't get buried.

"Yes," he said quietly. "*That* Jewel."

"Well, I'll be damned. How'd you pull that off, big brother? Flash her your pearly whites and Lawson charm?"

"Not funny, Alyse."

"Look, just do it right, okay? You don't have the best track record, if you know what I mean. There are a lot of broken hearts in your wake." She paused. "I want you to be happy, brother of mine. I really do. I know you put up a good front after Ana, but I also know that she hurt you. Bad. I want you to have someone in your life that means something. That's there for you, in your corner. Work can't be everything. Dad is a perfect example of that. He's rich, success-ful, feared and completely alone. All the success and money in the world can't keep you warm at night or fix the things inside you that are broken."

"Psychology 101," he playfully snarked. Although the imploding of his relationship with Ana had covered all of the tabloids for weeks, that was the tip of the iceberg when it came to the women who had come and gone in his life. The only upside was that the world didn't chronicle all of those de-tails.

"Whatever. But I'm serious." She pushed

out a breath. "Anyway, the other reason for my call was to invite you to dinner. Myles is in town for a week, and you promised we would all get together."

"Fine," he conceded. "When?"

"How's tomorrow night."

"It doesn't sound like a question."

"It's not. Brad will be there, and Myles is bringing his new girlfriend — Jessica, I think her name is. You should bring Jewel. I'd love to meet her and talk about her work."

"Aw, I don't know about that."

"Think about it. I swear I'll be on my best behavior."

Craig chuckled. "Highly unlikely, but I'll think about it. I'm not promising anything."

"See you tomorrow. Eight. Love you," she said before he could get a word in.

He placed the phone on the nightstand. It was nearly eleven. He was too tired to drive over to see Jewel, but he wouldn't let the night end without talking with her.

He knew what he felt for her was way beyond what he'd thought it would be. He'd only known her for a matter of weeks, but it felt as if she had always been a part of his life. When they talked it was easy. They laughed, they listened, they shared.

She told him what it was like growing up without a mother and how her father worked so hard to make it up to her and ensure that her dream to become an artist was realized. She went to the best schools, traveled and made a name for herself in the art world, and her father had been with her every step of the way, never asking for anything in return except that she be happy.

The only thing they'd ever bumped heads about, she'd said, was her ex, Simon. Her father had never liked him, didn't trust him, said he was a charmer — and not in a complimentary way. He'd been right, and the breakup took more out of her than she realized; compounded with her father's then escalating illness, she never really recovered. Her father was her reason for everything. She wanted to thank him for all that he had done, so she'd worked tirelessly to make him proud, to pay back the debt of gratitude, and so she barely hesitated when she realized that she would have to give up her career because her father needed her. She hinted at the degree of his illness, only saying that he needed twenty-four-hour care, which was why she'd given up her career, which ultimately led to her dire financial situation. But she said no matter what, she would not have done anything differently.

It was that selfless attitude that he so admired in Jewel. Her depth of caring was like nothing that he had experienced. His father was the polar opposite. To show that you cared was a sign of weakness in Jake Lawson's book, and weakness was unacceptable. But it was more than that. His father's vehement disdain for what Craig chose for a living was totally irrational. He knew that it had something to do with his mother, but he never knew exactly what that was. And if anyone else in the family knew they never told him.

He would make himself crazy going in circles about his father. He reached for the phone and called Jewel. He knew that the sound of her voice would quell the questions and quiet the unending storm within him.

Much to his surprise, he asked and Jewel agreed. Even more surprising was that his baby sis actually kept her promise and behaved.

Dinner was a fun-filled event, with Myles and Alyse vying for the best recounting of their childhood antics. Alyse's new beau was a corporate attorney on the partnership track, and Myles's latest was, of course, a model. He was, of all the Lawson clan, a mirror of their cousin Rafe. Women generally tumbled over themselves to get to

Myles, and he'd charm them with his good looks, unavailable demeanor and good old Southern charisma. It was a quality that all of the Lawson men shared. They believed in making a woman feel like a queen.

Alyse and Jewel got on as if they had been friends for years. He got a little jumpy when Alyse whisked Jewel away into the other room, but later found out that Alyse wanted Jewel's opinion on a piece of art that she was thinking of purchasing. Had Alyse asked that question weeks ago, he was sure that Jewel's response would have been quite different. Now that she'd started painting again, her love of the arts had been re-ignited, and talking about it only fueled her fire. He hoped that in time she would consider showing her work again. But one step at a time.

"I really like your sister and brother," Jewel said as they headed back to her place in Craig's Suburban. "Brad seems like a nice guy, and your brother's girlfriend is stunning, to say the least."

"They liked you, too."

Jewel grinned. "I loved the stories about you guys growing up. I have no idea what it's like to have siblings. You're lucky."

A warmth spread inside him. "Yeah, I

guess I am." He turned to her and grinned. "I don't think I realized how much I missed them," he said in a faraway voice. "We were really close."

"You still can be."

"That's pretty hard."

"Only as hard as you make it. You have the means to travel at a moment's notice. You can offer to fly them out to where you are for visits. You can make it a point to come home for holidays."

He pulled onto her street. "You want me to stay?" he asked, smoothly switching topics.

"Of course. But don't think you've gotten away from what we were talking about," she said with a knowing arch of her brow.

"Yes, ma'am." He leaned over and gave her a quick kiss of acquiescence.

A frantic banging on her bedroom door jerked Jewel and Craig out of a deep sleep. Jewel leaped up, disoriented. The banging came again, along with the wailing of her name. She jumped out of bed, grabbed her robe and ran to the door.

She tugged it open with her heart pounding. "Minerva, what is it? What's wrong?"

"Oh, God. Oh, God. I went to check on him and he wasn't in his room! I looked everywhere." She squeezed Jewel's arms.

"What! What are you saying? He has to be here." She shoved her arms into the sleeves of her robe. Waves of hysteria began to build.

"Jewel, what is it?" Craig asked from the shadows of the room.

"My father. He's not in his room." She turned to dart out.

"I'm coming with you." He grabbed his clothes from the floor and quickly got dressed. Minerva was already halfway down the hall.

The trio fanned out in the house, searched every room, every crawl space, but it was Craig who discovered the back door was not locked and partially open.

"You have flashlights?" he asked.

"In the drawer near the sink," Minerva said and hurried to get it.

"Oh, no, if he's gone outside . . ." Jewel's voice disintegrated into terror.

"We'll find him, and everything is going to be all right. I promise."

Jewel beat back tears with rapid blinks of her eyes. She nodded. "Stay here, Minerva, in case Daddy wanders back," she instructed then followed Craig out onto the back of the property.

Jewel and Craig combed every inch of the

property, and more than an hour later they still had not found her father. Jewel was beyond frantic.

Craig held her tight. "Baby, we need to call the police."

She nodded her head against his chest. Together they returned to the house, and Jewel made the call.

While they waited for the arrival of the police, Jewel finally told him the full story of her father's illness.

"He suffers with an aggressive form of Alzheimer's and dementia. Medication worked for a while, until it didn't. We tried everything. Every doctor. Nothing worked." Tears slid down her cheeks. "They told me I would have to put him in an institution so that he could be cared for. My father! I couldn't do that. I wouldn't. After the debacle in New York, he got worse, and I'd lost my confidence. It made sense to put that part of our lives behind us and move to whatever this new one held. I took on caring for him full-time." She swallowed. "Until it got to be too much. That's when I hired Minerva. At first she would come during the day, but after about a year she started staying longer . . . into the night, until it was twenty-four hours a day." She lowered her head. Craig clutched her hand.

She drew in a shuddering breath. "We were on the verge of losing the house," she whispered. "I'd all but exhausted my earnings, ate into my savings. And then like magic, you came along." She laughed sadly and sniffed back tears. "I thought, *a miracle.* But then I met you, and I looked into your eyes and you turned my world upside down. I didn't want to risk caring about and losing anyone else, even at the thought of losing the house. So I said no. I was scared." Her voice wobbled. "It was Minerva that told me to take a chance on being happy . . . even if it was only for a little while."

"It doesn't have to be," he blurted out. "I don't want it to be. I'm in love with you. Crazy in love with you."

"You . . . you love me?"

"With every ounce of my being." He leaned over and kissed her with all of the love that had burst from his soul. "We can make it work," he said against her lips.

"How?" she whispered through her tears.

"We'll find a way."

The lights from the police car lit up the lawn.

"I promise," he said before they ran down to meet the officers and Jewel gave a description of her father.

The trio waited in frightened silence for some word from the police. It was more than an hour later when the officers returned with Augustus in tow. He'd wandered nearly a mile away and had fallen asleep. He was disheveled and totally disoriented, even lashing out at Jewel, which broke her heart into a million pieces. Oddly, it was Craig who was able to soothe him, talk to him in quiet tones and get him cleaned up and back to bed.

By the time Augustus was settled and asleep, they were all beyond exhausted. Daybreak was on the horizon.

"I don't want to leave, but I have to get back. We have an early shoot in town. Will you be okay?"

"Go. I'll be fine." She looked into his eyes. "I can't thank you enough for everything that you did."

"There's no need to thank me for anything. Whatever you need, whenever you need it." He turned to leave.

"Craig . . ."

He stopped and turned back.

"I love you," she whispered.

He smiled. "I needed that."

She hugged herself and watched him hurry away.

CHAPTER 14

The filming in town took another two weeks to complete. Craig was beyond busy. As much as he hated it, there was little time to spend with Jewel, but he made it a point to check in with her every day and ask about her father.

The experience that night and seeing the depth of her love for her dad and all that she had sacrificed for him forced him to rethink his relationship with his own father and the importance of family. Even if his father couldn't put his personal issues aside, Craig knew he had to make one last effort, swallow his pride and confront his father.

He was a grown, successful, independent man, but when he pulled up in front of his father's palatial estate — his childhood home — he felt like a child again. He'd thought about calling first, but he knew that if his father wouldn't speak to him, it would be the final break. After debating the wisdom of what he was about to do, he finally got out of his car and went to the front door.

The last person he expected to answer was his father.

"Dad."

The stunned expression on Jake Lawson's face spoke volumes. The ten years since he'd last seen his father showed in the slope of Jake's broad shoulders, the dimming of his once piercing gaze and the firm mouth that had softened.

"Craig . . ."

Did his voice crack with emotion, or did Craig only imagine it?

"I, uh, was in town . . . I wanted to see you."

An uncomfortable silence hung between them.

"I suppose you should come in then," he finally said. He opened the door wider and stepped aside.

Craig walked in, took a look around, and the past rushed at him like a speeding train, the good and the ugly. He turned toward his father, who still stood at the door.

Jake extended a hand toward the living area. Craig led the way and took a seat on the couch. He rested his arms on his thighs.

"Drink? Bourbon, if I remember."

"Thanks. Yes."

Jake walked over to the bar, and that's when Craig noticed the slowing of his father's once purposeful step. He was getting old. He had more years behind him than in front of him. The realization shook him.

Jake returned with two glasses and handed one to Craig. He slowly lowered himself into an armchair.

"I saw the write-up about you and this film of yours in the papers."

The corner of Craig's mouth lifted in a smile. "Yeah, we're just about finished."

Jake took a swallow of his drink.

"I understand it's about the family."

"Not entirely. It's based on the family, or a family like ours, the struggle from nothing to prominence and success."

"I suppose you'll be going back to Europe when you're done."

"Not right away."

"Hmm." He took another swallow. "So what brings you here after all this time . . . to see me?"

Craig hesitated. What he was about to say could go either way. "I've been doing a lot of thinking, a lot of soul searching. I know that you don't think much of what I do. I'll never fully understand it, but I . . . want my father back. Life is so short. We've spent the past ten years not speaking to each other. Years that we can never get back. I've always respected you and all of your success, and I understand that you only wanted the best for me, for all of us. But I'm not you. I'll never be you. All I've ever wanted was for you to respect *my* dreams. And maybe, just maybe be happy for me, that I've achieved them. It's what you taught me. Go after what I want. That has got to mean something, Dad."

Jake lifted his chin and looked away.

"Just tell me. Now, finally. Why?"

"It was your mother's dream, too," he said slowly, reaching back in time. "She was good. They said she could be great, and I was her biggest cheerleader."

Craig watched his father's throat work up and down.

"That night . . . of the accident. She told me she had a last-minute rehearsal and she'd be back late." He pressed his lips together, and Craig could see the pain of the past race across his father's face. "She didn't have a rehearsal. She was with him."

"Him? Who?" His heart began to pound.

"Her leading man." He snorted a laugh. "They'd been having an affair for months. She was going to leave me — us." His voice grew hard. "He was in the car with her that night. He was driving. She was killed on impact. He survived for about three hours."

"But you always told us that Mom was in the car alone," he said, the shock not registering.

"I did it to protect all of you. Back then there wasn't all of this social media bull crap. Your uncle Branford pulled some strings and had the whole thing covered up. We couldn't have that kind of scandal."

Craig felt sick. The vague image that he'd had of his mother was forever tarnished. Now it all made ugly, terrible sense.

"I wanted to keep you as far away from that life as possible, and when you told me that you were going to be a filmmaker, all I could think was that it would take you away the same way it did her. It may not make sense to you. It may never make sense to you, but I didn't want to lose you, too." His voice shook. "But I did anyway. There was nothing I could do to stop you."

"Why didn't you tell me, Dad? All these years."

"I . . . wanted you to keep the memory that you had of your mother, not the one that I had." He hung his head. His shoulders shook with all the years of grief, and loneliness and loss.

Craig jumped up and went to kneel at his

233

side. He put his arms around his father and held him as he wept.

"Oh, my God, Craig, I'm so sorry," Jewel said as she lay next to him in bed. She stroked his hair. "I can't imagine what your father must have felt."

"He loved her. That I know for sure," he said into the darkness. "I remember when I was little how he used to touch her and light up every time she came into the room, how he'd steal a kiss whenever he thought we weren't looking. And I thought, *I want to have what they have when I grow up.* Humph — it was all a sham."

"I don't believe that. I'm sure your mother loved him. She had three children with him, built a life with him. That has to count for something. Don't dismiss that. Sometimes . . . things change and cloud our vision for a time, but it doesn't make the past go away."

"I don't know," he said sadly. "Maybe you're right. The worst part is he and I spent all this time being at each other's throats when we could have been each other's ally."

"Now you have the opportunity to work on things between you." She paused. "There is one thing that I want to say, and then I'm going to let it go."

"What's that?"

"Don't shift the animosity that you felt for your father onto your mother. Forgive her. Remember the mother that she was to you. Don't take on a new demon."

He turned fully onto his side to face her and ran his finger down the bridge of her nose. "How did you get so wise?"

"My dad was a great teacher."

"I love you, Jewel Fontaine."

"I totally believe that."

"I gotta run, baby," Craig said the following morning. "Loose ends to tie up."

Jewel sat on the side of the bed and watched him get dressed. "When will you be totally finished?" she asked with trepidation.

He stopped. "Tomorrow."

Her heart sank. "When were you going to tell me?"

"Tonight." He looked sheepish. He came to sit next to her. "I know I should've said something, but the moment I did, it would make it real. I kept thinking I could drag out the inevitable."

She pushed up from the bed and crossed the room. "We both knew you wouldn't be here forever. It had to come to an end at some point." She kept her back to him.

Craig came up behind her. He slid his arms around her waist. "I promised you that we would work it out, that I'd find a way. I meant that."

She didn't respond. He kissed the back of her neck.

"We'll talk tonight."

And then he was gone.

Throughout the day Jewel continued to remind herself that she was prepared for this. She'd known the day would come when he would have to go back to his life. She'd wanted to believe that somehow he could make the impossible possible, but if nothing else she was a realist. Their brief idyll was coming to a close. If their love was a script, she wondered how Craig would pen their ending.

Then another reality pressed to the forefront. The money that she'd been paid for the use of the house wouldn't last forever. It would get them through the summer and maybe early fall. Her small baking business, such as it was, wouldn't fill the gap.

She looked around at the canvases in various stages of completion, and an idea hit her. She went for her phone and called Mai Ling. They hadn't spoken in months. Jewel was sure that Mai was tired of trying to convince her to get back to work, to put a small show together. Since the days of working as Jewel's personal assistant, Mai had moved on to running her own publicity office. Mai knew the movers and shakers in the Big Easy and beyond.

Jewel tugged on her bottom lip with her teeth as she listened to the phone ring.

"Mai Ling and Associates. How may I help you?"

"Hello. This is Jewel Fontaine. Is Mai available?"

"Hold one moment."

Jewel had barely sat down when Mai's voice screamed in her ear.

"Jewel! Jewel! Girl. How are you? Oh, my goodness, I was just thinking of you. Are you okay? Dad?"

"Everything is fine. How are you?"

"Crazy busy. But I'd rather be busy with you, as you well know."

"Maybe you will."

"Wait . . . what are you saying? Don't play."

Jewel giggled. She hadn't realized how much she'd missed her friend. "I'm not. Do you have some time today to stop by the house? There's something I want to show you, then we can talk."

"I'm putting the rest of my day on hold. Be there in a half hour."

"Mai, you are still crazy."

"Yep! See ya soon."

" 'Kay."

Jewel disconnected the call, feeling better than she'd felt in hours. A new energy flowed through her veins, an excitement that she hadn't felt in years. She didn't want to get her hopes up. Mai would be brutally honest with her, that much she knew for sure. Then she would decide.

Mai must have taken a jet, because she'd made the thirty-minute trip in record time.

"Oh, Jewel, it's so good to see you," Mai said, hugging her friend. She stepped back and held her at arm's length. She angled her head to the side. "There's something glowing around you. You got a new man?"

Jewel tossed her head back and laughed. "We'll talk over wine and lunch. But first . . ." She took Mai's hand and led her out of the house and over to the studio. "I need you to be honest," she warned before she opened the door.

"Jewel," she whispered, the reality of what was happening beginning to hit home. "You . . . you've been working?" Her sloped eyes grew wide.

"Just come inside."

They stepped in, and Jewel came around the back of the canvas to the front. Mai followed.

Her gasps were confirmation. Mai moved reverently from one canvas to the next. "My God, Jewel . . . these are magnificent." She whirled toward her friend. "Phenomenal." She turned back to the renderings. "They tell a story," she said in awe, studying each one carefully.

"It's the story of *Rendezvous With Destiny* captured on canvas."

Mai frowned. "You mean the film that everyone's been talking about?"

Jewel nodded.

"Yes! Of course, you had a front-row seat."

"These are some of the scenes from the film, but what I wanted to do was to recreate the feeling of the time as well."

"Girl, you did that in spades. These are . . . I'm at a loss. Tell me you're going to show them."

"That's what I want to talk with you about."

"Consider it done. You know I have my contacts. We won't start off with anything big. Something local, to get the buzz going." Her brows rose to peaks. "They would be perfect publicity for the film! Maybe we could partner with the production company. I'm thinking if you had them filming on your property, you have some kind of connection."

Jewel gave a sly grin. "Something like that."

"Now I need that drink. This could be major. I mean, really major."

Jewel was on a natural high by the time Mai left. Her head was filled with limitless possibility. There was still so much more to do. For a show, even a small one, she would need at least five more pieces. They would need to be sealed and framed.

She felt that she had purpose again. That what she loved about herself wasn't really lost at all. And it took Craig walking into her life . . . and now walking out for her to find herself again. She supposed that even though there would be a void in her life once Craig returned to Europe, she would still have her art.

This time she believed that she was made of more resilient stuff and could take whatever the critics threw her way without crumbling, plus she had Minerva in her life to help with her father.

She took one last look at the row of renderings. She had her mojo back.

CHAPTER 15

"So what are you gonna do, man?" Anthony asked over drinks with Craig.

Craig stared into his glass. "Been trying to figure it out." He angled his head toward Anthony. "I can't ask her to run around the world with me. She has her father to think about. And I can't very well stay behind. We have projects lined up for the next two years."

"Yeah, and so where does that leave you?"

"Screwed."

"Listen, plenty of folks have done the long-distance thing. If it's meant to work out, it will. What is she saying?"

"Not much. It was me that told her I'd find a way."

"Humph." Anthony took a swallow of his drink. "Well, then, my brother, I suggest you get to finding a way."

"Thanks," he said sarcastically.

"Hey, I'm really glad to hear about you

241

and your pops, man." He clapped Craig on the back. "I know how much that thing between you ate you up, even if you didn't admit it. Good that y'all made peace. I can't imagine how hard that must have been to hear all that, and even harder for your pop to tell it to you."

"Yeah, it's gonna take some time to get past it. But I'm planning to take Jewel's advice and not shift my animosity from my dad to my mom. It's a no-win situation."

"I hear that. Smart lady."

Craig half grinned. "Yeah."

"You know, if you need to, you can hang back a couple more days. I can take care of the crew and get started on the editing back in LA."

"Thanks, man. I might take you up on that. I'll let you know in the morning." He lifted his cell from the table and checked the time. "I'm going to cut out. Stop by and see Jewel."

"Cool."

They gripped hands and shoulder hugged.

"See you in the morning," Craig said and walked out.

On the drive over to Jewel's place, he went through a dozen scenarios. None of them was going to solve their problem, and he wasn't sure what would. When he rolled up to the front of the property, he called. She answered on the second ring.

"Hey, baby. I'm out front."

"I'm at the cottage."

"Be there in a few."

At least she didn't sound as upset as she'd looked this morning. If anything she sounded happy.

Jewel met him at the door with open arms and a welcoming smile. "Hey," she whispered and stepped into his arms.

"Hey, yourself." He squeezed her close.

"Come on in. How did it go today?"

"Good. It's a wrap," he joked.

"I want to talk to you, and there's something I need to show you."

She led him inside. On the evenings they spent at the cottage, Jewel made it a point to keep the canvases covered, insisting that she never showed anyone her work while it was in progress. It was partly true, but in this case she was more concerned about how Craig would feel about the work. If he felt that the art truly depicted his vision.

They walked around to the front of the canvases, and one by one Jewel removed the cloths that covered them until all four were revealed.

For several moments Craig was completely

speechless. Slowly he walked back and forth in front of them. Then he spun toward her. His face looked as if it was lit from within. His eyes actually glowed.

"Jewel, these pictures . . . they're . . ."

"Do you like them?"

"Like them? I love them. They're amazing, even more stunning than watching it on film. The way you captured the nuances of their expressions, the body language — they look as if any minute they're going to walk off the canvas and into the room."

He looked at her with awe. "You are incredible. This is what you've been working on and hiding from me?"

She grinned. "Yes. I didn't know how they would turn out or how you would feel about them."

"You don't plan to hide them in here forever, do you? You *are* planning to show them?"

"That's the part I wanted to talk with you about . . ."

Craig listened intently to what Jewel and her friend Mai had envisioned, and his own mind was on overdrive thinking of the collaborative potential.

"We can do this," he cut in before she'd finished. "I love the idea. We use your art as publicity for the movie and the movie as publicity for your art. It's crazy brilliant, and I know it'll work."

Jewel breathed a deep sigh of relief. "I wasn't sure if you would go for it."

"Whatever can keep us and bring us closer together, then I'm all for it, baby. This may open up the doors to a whole new way of cross advertising, not to mention the business it will bring you."

Jewel plopped down on a chair and looked at him. "I hadn't even thought about that," she said with wonder in her voice.

"Yeah, well, think about it, 'cause I believe that you have taken your art to a whole new level. This is just the beginning."

She leaped up and jumped into his arms, wrapping her legs around his waist. "I love you, love you." She kissed him solidly on the mouth.

"Love you right back, baby. Why don't you let me show you how much?"

"I'm liking the sound of that."

"I was supposed to leave tomorrow, but I can stay on a couple more days," Craig said against Jewel's neck.

She draped a leg across his body. "It's okay. We'll be okay. I was thinking that maybe I could come out to LA in a few weeks for a long weekend."

"You'd do that?"

"Yes. Of course."

He hugged her tighter. "You just let me know when you're ready and I'll take care of everything."

"No arguments from me," she joked.

"And I'll come to you before I head back to London, and when I get there I'll send for you. You can come and see me work on my next project, maybe get some inspiration," he added and slid his hand down between her legs.

"I'm inspired already," she said against his mouth.

"We're going to make this work, baby," he said, rolling on top of her. "Whatever it takes."

"Show me just how invested you are in our success."

"With pleasure."

"You sure you don't want me to ride with you to the airport?" Jewel asked the following morning.

"No, that's only going to make it harder."

"We'll see each other in two weeks."

Jewel heaved a sigh.

Craig hesitated a moment, but he knew what was on his mind had to be said.

"There is one thing that was bugging me about your work."

"What?"

"If we're going to do this together, then you can't have a show of the work this far in advance of the release of the film."

Her body tensed. "Why? It's my work."

"I understand that, but it's based on *my* film."

"So what are you saying? I thought you loved the concept. You were all for it a minute ago, now it's *your* film."

Craig pushed out a breath. He'd been stung in the past, in his early days of screenwriting, when a woman he was dating took full credit for a project that they'd worked on together based on his idea. He looked at the hurt that masked Jewel's face. That was then — this was now.

"What I mean is if you show it too far in advance, it will dilute their value in relation to the movie and they won't do the movie any good at all. This whole thing has to be timed."

The only thing she'd been focused on was that she'd finished a set of work that she was proud of, work that was gallery ready. Gallery ready meant income — an income that she sorely needed.

Craig walked up to her and held her upper arms. She looked in his eyes.

"If we're going to do this, we need to plan it right, that's all I'm saying. I want this to work. Talk with your friend Mai and see what she says. But as far as I see it, too early is too soon." He pecked her on the lips then hung on for a real kiss. "I'll call you when I land," he said. "Love you." He pecked her lips again, turned and hurried out.

Jewel paced the room. This was her work. She'd come to him with the idea. Sure, the inspiration came from the film, but the work was hers. She'd stayed in the shadows and sat on the sidelines long enough. It was her time again.

"I hadn't thought of that," Mai said thoughtfully as she sat opposite Jewel at the kitchen table. "When is the film being released?"

"At least six months from now. I'm pretty sure he'll take it to film festivals before it's released in theaters."

"That may work." She put down her coffee cup. "Look, this is a stumbling block, not the end of the journey. I know you had it in your head to jump feetfirst. But this may be a blessing in disguise." Her eyes lit. She leaned forward. "You will still need at least five to seven more pieces to complete the series."

"Right."

"The film has to do what it has to do in the next few months, but in the meantime, I start building your brand. Leaking information of your comeback. Hinting at a major collaboration that's a game changer for the industry. We get you ready. You get your work ready, and launch the film and your art at the earliest film festival."

Jewel got excited again. "That might work."

"Not might, *will*!"

They lifted their coffee cups in salute.

As promised, the moment Craig landed in LA he called Jewel while he waited for his bags. Although they did the hug and kiss thing and said the *I love you*s, he'd still left not feeling good about things between them. He was thrilled that Jewel had gotten her inspiration back, and having gotten it from the film made the connection between them even tighter. It was like two creative minds thinking as one. That itself was a turn-on. The very idea that she was able to see beyond what he presented and translate that into art blew him away.

If only it was that simple. Two creative minds were bound to clash. They each had their vision, their purpose. That was the crossroads where he and Jewel now stood.

When they'd faced each other in the cottage, he knew the instant the words were out of his mouth that she didn't agree. It wasn't what she wanted. And he understood why, but he also had to consider what he wanted and what would best serve him and the film.

He'd run the concept past Anthony on the plane ride and he was totally on board but agreed that too soon would blow a hole in the entire project.

Somehow they had to come to a compromise.

"Hey, baby," he said when she picked up. "I know it's late."

"I was waiting for your call," she said sleepily. "How was the flight?"

"No problems." He paused, cleared his throat. "Hey, listen, about this whole art meets film. I don't want to get in your way. I know how important your work is to you, just like mine is to me. I can't let what I want stop you. I've lived through that with my father. I know what it did to me, what it did to him, and I would never put that on you. You deserve your moment. So if you want to put a show together, whatever you want to do, I'm behind you."

He didn't know at what point he'd changed his mind. Maybe it was when he heard her voice, or remembered the look in her eyes, or maybe he was finally seeing that to love someone was more than just a feeling — it was doing. Whatever the reason, he was glad that he did.

"That's why I love you," she said softly. "But neither of us has to put our work on hold. Mai and I talked about it today, and we think this will work." She went on to tell them what they'd discussed and how they would gradually release the work.

"Brilliant! Absolutely brilliant. That'll work. The first showing is the Independent Film Festival, then Sundance in January and Cannes in May. Distribution is key, but I don't see a problem. We can plan on a release after Labor Day but definitely before Christmas to even be considered for a Golden Globe or SAG. I'll have to press my people, but I know we can get the film ready in time."

Jewel breathed a sigh of relief. "I'm so happy."

"I miss you already," he said in response. "Let me know when you want to come out. I'll make all of the arrangements."

"I will." She yawned.

"Get some rest. We'll talk tomorrow."

"Okay." She yawned again.

"I love you," he said.

"I love you, too."

"Good night, baby."

"Night."

Craig slid the phone in his pocket and strode out of the airport baggage area and into the waiting car. Electric energy pumped through his veins. He could see an amazing future spread out in front of him, and Jewel was right at his side.

CHAPTER 16

The next few months were a whirlwind of activity. Jewel worked every day perfecting her pieces, and bit by bit the collection grew to an astonishing body of work that replicated the film in a way that was surreal. She worked from many of the photographs that Norm had taken and from the sketches she'd done while watching the film unfold on the grounds and in the house.

She was in constant touch with Mai, who dropped in at least once per week to check on Jewel's progress and to update her on her publicity plans, which had begun to roll out. News stations and several key art magazines had been in touch wanting interviews. "We've got them in the bag," Mai had said, "but time is key."

In between Jewel spent as much time as she could with her father, who seemed to grow more and more frail with each passing day. There were times when she would come into his room and see him sitting by the window and he'd remind her of a broken sparrow, trapped on the ground and unable to fly. The vibrant, robust man of her youth was gone. In his place was the shell of her father.

It was her fear and concern for her father that held her back from taking the trip to London to spend some time with Craig and cut short her visit to New York, where he'd gone to do some of the talk shows. She worried constantly that something would happen and she wouldn't be there for her father. There were nights when she would jerk out of her sleep thinking he'd gotten out of the house again. The idea that she would have to leave him for any length of time grew to be less and less of a possibility each day. But the first showings of the work and the film were happening within a week at the Indie Film Festival, then Cannes and Sundance. She didn't know if she would be at any of them.

"Hey, Daddy," she said softly and crossed the room to where he sat by the window. She took a seat. "How are you today? It's beautiful outside. You want to go for a walk?"

He looked across at her with a faraway expression on his face. He smiled. "You're a pretty little gal."

Jewel's heart knocked. "Come on, let's go outside."

Once outside, Jewel held on tightly to her father's thin arm, and they strolled slowly across the glistening green grass of the backyard.

"I had so much fun running around out here when I was little. Do you remember the time when I climbed that tree, the one right over there?" She pointed to the giant maple that was the centerpiece of the property. "Got halfway up and got scared. Couldn't move. Wouldn't go up and couldn't come down." She chuckled at the memory. "You were the one that coaxed me down." She squeezed his arm and rested her head on his shoulder. "You climbed up and sat with me, talked with me, told me how proud you were because I was so fearless, that I could do anything, and no matter what you would always be there cheering me on." Tears rolled down her cheeks. "You held my hand, and we came down the tree together." She sniffed. "You were always there, like I am now."

"I had my time," he said.

The strength and clarity in his voice brought Jewel up short. She held her breath.

"It's your time, baby girl. Time for you to

climb down on your own, spread your wings with that nice fella. I'll cheer you on from the sidelines."

She looked into his face and knew that in that moment, he saw her. Really saw her, and his words weren't some out-of-context ramblings. He was here in the moment with her. Her throat knotted. She wrapped her arms around her father and held on, needing to secure this moment between them just a little while longer. When she finally released him and stepped back to look into his eyes, he was already gone.

The first article on the return of Jewel Fontaine hit the newsstand a month before the Indie Film Festival. And in the following months, she was on the covers of *Art Noir, Contemporary Art, People,* and *Cosmo.* She appeared with Craig on the *Today* show and E! to talk about their collaboration without giving too much away. The film and the art worlds were buzzing, and Jewel's phone wouldn't stop ringing.

Craig returned to New Orleans for two weeks and they spent the entire time in bed together to make up for lost time.

"This is all so crazy," Jewel said the morning Craig was preparing to leave for LA. "I never thought I'd be in this place again."

She looked at him, and for the first time all the excitement turned to doubt. "All the traveling and reporters and people wanting to know everything about me . . . you." She sighed and shook her head. "I left all that madness behind and settled for a different kind of life." She looked at him. "I'd gotten used to it. To the normalcy of it. Sure, it was hard financially, and then you came into my life and changed all that, but . . ."

Craig sat next to her. He lifted a stray curl from her face and tucked it behind her ear. "So what are you saying?"

"I don't know what I'm saying." Her eyes pleaded with him to understand. She lowered her head.

"You've been down this road. You know what it's like under the spotlight."

She shook her head back and forth. "Not like this."

Craig blew out a breath. "All this craziness is the prelim. Once the film hits, the noise will die down and we can go back to being Jewel and Craig." He captured her hand in his. His eyes ran over her face. "I got you," he said. "We're going to do this together. I promise you."

All at once that day in the tree so long ago, when her dad climbed up to get her and assured her that it was going to be all right, flooded her thoughts and warmed her heart. And all those years later under that very same tree he gave her wings and told her to fly. It was exactly what Craig was doing.

She pressed her head against Craig's chest and shut her eyes. "Thank you, Daddy," she whispered.

CHAPTER 17

After much prayer and having her arm twisted by Minerva, Jewel set out with Craig to set fire to the industry. Just as Mai predicted, the unveiling of Jewel's first piece at the Indie Film Festival was a phenomenal success, which only upped the ante for the festivals to follow. Jewel and Craig were bombarded by journalists and photographers, all wanting to know every detail of their lives and their collaboration and to capture every moment.

Just as he'd promised, Craig was with Jewel every step of the way. It had been a while since she'd been under the glare of the spotlight, but with Craig by her side she glided instead of stumbled, and before long it was second nature again.

The biggest coup was the early premieres at targeted theaters. At the end the audiences actually stood for a good five minutes, shouting, applauding and stomping their approval. Upon their exit from the theater, the lobby was lined with Jewel's art, which served as the nightcap of the evening and reinforced the audience's theater experience.

The reviews were stellar, one after the other touting the brilliance of the film and the creative genius of the art. The pairing of the two had set the marketing world on its ear. Things only got better when Craig was nominated for a Golden Globe for best picture and best director. And he was informed that Milan Chase received a nomination for best actress.

Jewel leaped up into his arms and squealed with delight the minute he put the phone down.

"Oh, my God. This is so wonderful! Congratulations, baby." She kissed him long and hard. "You deserve this." She caressed his face. "So proud of you."

"We did this. Me and you. Don't ever think otherwise," he said, looking deep into her eyes. "It was your home that set the tone. That meant everything. And your renderings bring it all together. We did this."

She grinned. "If you say so, Mr. Golden Globe nominee."

"I want you there."

"Where?"

"At the Globes."

"Really?"

"Yes, really." He cupped her face in his hand. "Every step of the way . . . together, me and you."

He hadn't spoken to Milan since they'd completed the final edits months earlier, he thought as he held Jewel close. She'd called and left messages on his cell phone, but he'd never called back. Now with her getting the nomination, they would be thrown back in each other's paths. Not a journey he was looking forward to taking.

"You can't turn down these interviews, man," Anthony admonished. "It's going to hurt your chances and the chances for the film. We open nationwide in a week. You have a major nomination along with your lead actress. People want to see you together."

Craig rocked his jaw and slowly paced the floor of his hotel suite.

"At least do one. *Entertainment Tonight.* They're fair and fun. It'll be easy. Besides, you've been able to keep your distance from Milan so far. You've been in the same cities on the same tours."

"Yeah, but the focus has never just been on me and her. It's not a good look, Tony.

There's no telling what Milan may say or do."

"Look, everything is taped. If she does something crazy, we get it cut out before it airs."

He turned to his longtime friend. "All right, tell them I'll do it. But I swear, if this thing goes to hell, I'm blaming you."

"Duly noted."

When Craig and Anthony arrived at the studio, they were swept into the green room, prepped and offered food and drink to bide their time.

"You have about a half hour before they get started. I'm going to check on a few things and I'll be back."

"Cool." He settled on the couch and plucked a grape from the bunch.

There was a knock at the door.

"Come on in."

The door eased open, and Milan stepped into his line of sight. He sat up on the couch. "Milan, what are you doing here?"

She stepped fully into the room and shut the door behind her. "I thought we should talk first."

"Really? About what?"

"About all the mess that has gone down between us." She sighed and folded her hands in front of her. "When we were together, whether you believe it or not, I really cared for you. Really. I knew I wasn't a big star or a famous model, I was just me. I used to pinch myself to be sure that I wasn't dreaming. Me, Milan Chase from Newark, New Jersey, in a relationship with you." She chuckled without humor. "I didn't think you would stay," she said. "I figured it was only a matter of time."

"You didn't have to lie to me, Milan."

She lowered her head. "I know. I know that now. But I thought if I told you that I was pregnant that you would stay with me."

"There never was a baby, Milan! You lied. I did care about you. I could have . . . maybe cared more. But what you did —" he shook his head "— was unforgivable. To lie and say that you lost it. To pretend to be devastated." He rubbed his face with his hands then looked up at her. "If I hadn't seen the text message from your partner in crime, Delys, I may have never known."

"I've said I'm sorry. It won't change what I did. I accept that, but what I came here to say was thank you."

"For what?"

"For giving me this chance, after all the shit I put you through. I know that you could have picked hundreds of other actors

263

for the part, but you chose me." Her voice wobbled.

"Because regardless of what you think, you are a helluva good actress. I saw that in you. I knew you could do this, and now you've proven to the world that you can. All you have to do now is have the same belief in yourself that I have in you. This is only the beginning, Milan. You have an amazing future ahead of you. But lies and backstabbing —" he shook his head "— will take you down."

She sniffed and smiled while trying not to cry. "They're going to have to redo my makeup."

He got up and crossed the room to stand in front of her. "You're a star. Go get the star treatment."

She leaned up and kissed his cheek. "Thank you." She walked out and straight into Anthony.

A look of panic crossed Anthony's face when he saw her wiping her eyes. "Everything cool?"

"Very," she said and hurried past him.

Anthony came in and shut the door. "What was that about?" he asked, hooking his thumb over his shoulder.

"Finally settling some old business. It's all good." He clapped Anthony on the back.

"Let's get this done. I need to go home to my woman."

CHAPTER 18

The night of the Golden Globe Awards was more spectacular than Jewel ever imagined. It took all of her good home training to keep her jaw from dropping every time she saw another star. And they were all there, from multiple award-winning actors to the newcomers. Not to mention the music royalty that fanned out among the well-heeled guests.

Craig had reserved two tables for the cast and his family. He was happy to see that Milan brought a date, and she seemed truly happy. Everyone was in place except for his father. It was more than he could have expected, but he had to try.

Since his visit, they'd spoken maybe twice. It was almost as if the conversation had never happened. His father had reverted back to his demeanor of indifference. But Craig would not let that steal his moment tonight.

Now that the film had opened and the full array of Jewel's art had been displayed, her phone would not stop ringing. Every producer and director on the East and West Coasts wanted to hire her to do renderings of their films and their actors. She was in such demand that she could pick and choose whom she wanted to work with. Never in a million years would she have thought that her personal passion would take her to this level. She and Craig had created a whole new genre of art. For well into the future she was financially solvent. The worries she'd had barely a year earlier were a thing of the past. And to add to her blessings, Alyse confided that after seeing the film and her art, she'd been looking into landmark designation for Jewel's home. She was getting some very positive feedback from the committee and the cachet of the Lawson name. But she swore Jewel to secrecy. If it came through, Jewel would never have to worry about the house again.

She squeezed Craig's hand. He turned to her. "I love you," she whispered. "No matter what happens tonight. You are *my* winner, and I'll prove it to you later."

"Wicked, wicked woman," he said against her mouth.

The evening's festivities were underway, and one after another presenters and winners took to the podium. The room overflowed with good cheer, laughter and plenty of food and drink. It was one big party.

The first of many wins for *Rendezvous With Destiny* kicked off with Milan Chase's win for best actress in a drama. She was so overcome she could barely get her words out as she looked onto the crowd of her contemporaries standing for her.

"There are so many people to thank, but one person stands out above them all. I must thank Craig Lawson, my director, my mentor, my friend. He believed in me when I didn't believe in myself and gave me an opportunity when I didn't deserve it. I'm standing here tonight because of him. Thank you." She raised her award above her head and was escorted off.

When his name was called for best director, it took several moments for it to register with him. His entire table was on its feet as he pulled himself together and jogged up the steps to the stage.

Jewel was certain she would simply burst

with pride and love as she watched him give his acceptance speech, and to see the love from his colleagues overflow and fill the room was overwhelming.

"There are so many people to thank. My entire crew, who work in front of and behind the scenes. The amazing actors who brought this story to life. I can't thank you enough. Hamilton and Milan, this is because of you," he said, lifting the statue. "But the one person that I have to thank and pay homage to is my lady, Jewel Fontaine. Her brilliance inspires me. Her beauty overwhelms me. Her selflessness taught me what it means to truly love another person. Without her I would be half the man I've become. And . . . if you'll have me, Jewel Fontaine, I want to spend the rest of my life with you working on the other half."

A collective gasp went up from the audience.

Jewel couldn't see for the tears that clouded her eyes. She stood and blew him kisses, mouthing, "Yes, yes, yes."

Craig grinned like a man finding a million bucks. "Now I'm a real winner. Thank you!"

He was escorted off the stage but held in the wings. The next category was best picture.

She said yes was all he could think about

as he stood on the side pacing back and forth. Visions of their life together played out in front of him. If he had to move back to Louisiana, he would. Whatever she wanted. Maybe he could purchase some property and set up a studio. What about kids? He wanted kids, lots of them, and the best part would be making them.

He was so engrossed in the swirl of his thoughts that it wasn't until the escort shook his arm to tell him they were calling his name did it register that he had won.

Craig walked back on stage in a semidaze. The lights, the people, the applause dazzled him. Best picture. It was the pinnacle of an artist's career.

For several moments he stood at the podium to pull himself together. He looked out at the crowd and found his table. The seat that had been empty wasn't any longer. His vision clouded for a moment. His father was there, clapping and nodding his approval. Craig nearly broke down, and it took all of his willpower to keep it together.

He wasn't sure what he said, if he said too little or too much. All he wanted to do was get off the stage and get to his family.

When Craig returned to the table, he was swarmed with hugs and kisses and handshakes. His father stood in front of him. Craig stood a step forward. Jake extended his hand, which Craig took. Jake pulled him into a tight bear hug. "I'm proud of you, son," he whispered. "I always have been." He clapped him heartily on the back then stepped back and gripped his shoulders. "I hear I'm getting a daughter-in-law."

Craig turned toward Jewel, and she stepped into his embrace. "Jewel, this is my dad, Jake Lawson."

"Oh, me and your dad are buddies. Right, Mr. Lawson?"

"When Alyse told me about the house, well . . . I thought it only right that I take a look from a real estate perspective."

"Your dad's been working with Alyse on the landmark designation," Jewel confessed.

"And, uh, no one was going to tell me?"

"Nope," they all said in unison.

"All this happiness and good news deserves a serious toast," Myles said and began filling glasses.

Jewel turned in to Craig's body so that they were only a breath apart. "I have something else to tell you."

"What?"

"I won't be doing any drinking or traveling for a while, and if you had a date in mind for a wedding . . . well, we may need to move it up."

He stared into her glowing face then down the curves of her body, hugged in a champagne-toned Vera Wang gown. "Jewel, are you telling me . . ."

"Twelve weeks. I wanted to wait to be sure. Are you happy?"

"Happy, baby — happy doesn't come close to what I'm feeling." He didn't care that they were in a room full of people and photographers. He pulled Jewel flush against him and kissed her as if they were the only two people in the world.

"I love you, girl," he hummed against her mouth to the applause of onlookers.

"I love you right back."

EPILOGUE

Jewel set up her easel and lined up the brushes and oils. The light coming in the window was perfect, and she wanted to capture it all.

Her father was in his favorite chair, and the morning sun seemed to put an extra spark in his eyes — or maybe it was holding his first granddaughter.

It didn't seem to matter when he would slip away and talk to Imani as if she was a tiny version of Jewel. When he would tell Imani stories of going into town to buy candy, or the hard days of working at the mill. It seemed perfectly all right. Because Imani needed to know about the past, her past, the history of where she'd come from. Who better to tell her than Granddad in his own special way?

Jewel worked quickly, sketching in charcoal to get the lines and angles, and when she was satisfied she began again following her drawing in oil.

Craig had just returned from working out a deal with his dad to purchase some property to open a production studio in town. He stood in the doorway of Augustus's bedroom watching the scene in front of him, frame by frame, stroke by stroke, generation to generation.

This moment, his family, *this* was a work of art that could never be duplicated. He'd searched for his place in the world. He'd traveled the globe looking to fill the emptiness inside him. And all along everything that he'd ever needed was right in his hometown, where it had been waiting for him all along. He could finally stop running.

Jewel glanced over her shoulder and stared into the eyes of the man she loved.

"Welcome home, baby."

ABOUT THE AUTHOR

Donna Hill began writing novels in 1990. Since that time she has had more than forty titles published, which include full-length novels and novellas. Two of her novels and one novella were adapted for television. She has won numerous awards for her body of work. She is also the editor of five novels, two of which were nominated for awards. She easily moves from romance to erotica, horror, comedy and women's fiction. She was the first recipient of the *RT Book Reviews* Trailblazer Award, won the *RT Book Reviews* Career Achievement Award and currently teaches writing at the Frederick Douglass Creative Arts Center.

Donna lives in Brooklyn with her family. Visit her website at donnahill.com.

The employees of Thorndike Press hope you have enjoyed this Large Print book. All our Thorndike, Wheeler, and Kennebec Large Print titles are designed for easy reading, and all our books are made to last. Other Thorndike Press Large Print books are available at your library, through selected bookstores, or directly from us.

For information about titles, please call:
  (800) 223-1244

or visit our Web site at:
  http://gale.cengage.com/thorndike

To share your comments, please write:
  Publisher
  Thorndike Press
  10 Water St., Suite 310
  Waterville, ME 04901